TRAITOR'S
BLACK ROSE

Paperback ISBN: 978-1-63337-853-7
Hardback ISBN: 978-1-63337-854-4
E-Book ISBN: 978-1-63337-855-1

Printed in the United States of America
1 3 5 7 9 10 8 6 4 2

TRAITOR'S BLACK ROSE

I.M. STOICUS

TABLE OF CONTENTS

DEDICATION

TRAITOR'S BLACK ROSE is dedicated to all those who have honorably served this Great Nation, as well as all patriots, God-fearing people, and advocates for our God-given Constitutional Rights. As Americans, we have accepted that all should be treated *equally under the eyes of the law*, and our legal system must adhere to the United States Constitution. We oppose any two-tier justice system or lawfare. I M Stoicus advocates for President Theodore Roosevelt's words: *"Patriotism means to stand by the country. It does not mean to stand by the president or any other public official, save exactly to the degree in which he himself stands by the country. It is patriotic to support him insofar as he efficiently serves the country. It is unpatriotic not to oppose him to the exact extent that by inefficiency or otherwise he fails in his duty to stand by the country. In either event, it is unpatriotic not to tell the truth, whether about the president or anyone else."*

1.

THE GLOBAL
DIVIDE

DURING A WELL-ATTENDED PRESIDENTIAL SPEECH at the site of the renewed Washington, DC, in Kansas, President Marcus Baros was at the presidential podium. It was a calm yet festive and patriotic summer day, Memorial Day in 2088.

He eloquently articulated, "We, as Americans, must continue to be the world's brilliant beacon of divine hope, prosperity, and God-given rights under a constitutional federal republic, as well as—"

His patriotic address was violently interrupted by a directed energy weapon (DEW) that obliterated landmarks, vehicles, and military equipment. In addition, three *fighterbots*, which are sophisticated military robots, attacked the unarmed, alarmed audience. This devastating assault murdered or injured several thousand presidential supporters. The calamity was a ghastly war zone; there was blood and mayhem everywhere. The presidential security detail immediately and effectively secured the president and his family; unfortunately, five heroic security guards sacrificed their lives to save others. Furthermore, other courageous individuals rose to the occasion and assisted victims in order to save their lives. In the aftermath, one of the president's secret servicemen found a *black rose* near a nationalist senator who was assassinated by one of the *fighterbots*. The secret serviceman reflected to himself: *This black rose is next to the body to remind us of our mortality, since it is a symbol of death.* The secret serviceman found another *black rose* with the United States flag in a triangular fold at the podium where the president was speaking, which is how the flag is presented to a loved one at a president's or military funeral. Unfortunately, the secret serviceman picked up the *black rose*, and he died instantly from poison. Another secret servicewoman, Mrs. Smith, who discovered the lifeless body of her comrade, pondered the words of Ayn Rand: **"To abstain from condemning a torturer is to become an accessory to the torture and murder of his victims."** *I swear to God that the murderer will pay for his or her crimes*, she thought.

The decisive United States Space Force (USSF) immediately vaporized the enemy satellite with a *directed laser beam (DLB)* weapon, as well as the three rogued *fighterbots*; rogued *fighterbots* are military robots that are not controlled by the sovereign. This, regrettably, was the third assassination attempt on the president's life. The two others were not known to the general public; however, his security detail and military were constantly on high alert. Fortunately, the president had been able to dodge the attempts. The assassins' failed attempts exemplified George Orwell's axiom that the assassins believed: **"Actions are held to be good or bad, not on their own merits, but according to who does them. There is almost no kind of outrage—torture, imprisonment without trial, assassination, the bombing of civilians—which does not change its moral color when it is committed by 'our' side."**

The belligerent globalist rebels were the usual suspects. They were also suspected of having assassinated President Baros's former vice president, Alfred Jones, and the vice president's wife, last year. This was, miserably, just one surreal example of how dreadful and violent the political divide had progressed in the United States and the world. The popular assassinated former vice president was a devoted nationalist and a four-star general with over thirty years of military service. Deceased Vice President Alfred Jones was the commanding general during the Venezuelan War. Unfortunately, there was no one held responsible for the assassination; the federal bureaucrats were claiming that the rogue satellite that killed the vice president had a computer malfunction, which no one seriously believed; most people suspected that the deep state was the guilty party.

Last year, *black roses* were mysteriously discovered at the grave of the vice president. While at the grave, the vice president's youngest child found the *black roses* but fortunately did not touch them. This was thanks to the secret servicewoman Mrs. Smith, who had previously discovered her departed colleague and prevented the child from touching the *black roses*. She had witnessed other assassination attempts of politicians who received *black roses*. As a result, the secret servicemen had been briefed for the past several months not to touch any *black roses*. The arguments of Eric Ambler, an English author, should be understood: **"The important thing to know about an assassination or an attempted assassination is not who fired the shot, but who paid for the bullet."**

Currently, the zeitgeist of the world was a political dichotomy of two adversarial camps: nationalists and globalists. Ex parte, the nationalist-controlled countries produced over 75 percent of the world's goods and services; these countries had a strong propensity toward laissez-faire free markets. The nationalist-controlled countries had less than 15 percent of the population who lived in poverty; additionally, their crime rate was less than a quarter of the globalist-controlled countries. The nationalist countries, with governmental leaders democratically elected, were comprised of federal republics and parliamentary forms of government with substantial human rights and capitalist tendencies. On the other hand, the globalist-controlled countries were tyrannical Marxist surveillance states with McCarthyist tendencies; these countries scrutinized their people with oppressive *policebots* and cameras. The globalist-controlled countries upheld George Orwell's observation: **"Power is not a means, it is an end. One does not establish a dictatorship in order to safeguard a revolution; one makes the revolution in order to establish the dictatorship."**

Based on his ethos, President Baros defined and ameliorated the Nationalist Party's philosophy and marketing; he understood that the party must stand for ideas other than mere anti-globalism and pro-nationalism. During his campaigns, he explained that the party ought to aim toward *FOCUS*, an acronym that stood for:

1. *Federal Republic*: States are sovereign and closer to the people, similar to how parents are closer and more caring to their children than a state or government would ever be.
2. *Orthodox*: We must advocate for American traditions, principles, and values.
3. *Constitution:* People's rights do not come from the government; the Constitution limits the federal government to guarantee individual rights.
4. *United*: Americans are united as lawful citizens, adhering to our constitution, laws, and values.

5. *Sacred*: We are one independent nation under our Creator.

President Baros advocated that a *federal republic* government allowed the states to be testing grounds for untested laws. In addition, it permitted individuals to live in the state that they preferred to be governed by. He expressed that the *orthodoxy* of America is a beacon of hope and success. The United States supported free markets, a constitutional government, and adherence to given rights that come from our Creator and not the government. Ironically, he believed a *Constitution* was necessary, since governments throughout the world tended to violate individual rights and tended to be tyrannical. The bureaucracy and deep state tended to believe that individuals were to be used for the government's ends, which President Baros adamantly disagreed with. He expressed that we as Americans do not agree with each other about everything; however, the American way of life and principles will continue to result in us being *united*. Finally, he accepted (which was highly controversial to the Globalist Party) that there was a *sacred* divine element to our nation, manifest destiny, and individuals. Finally, President Baros developed the acronym *FOCUS*, since too many people had become complacent throughout history, allowing many institutions to be taken over by the globalists. He believed that your plans must *FOCUS*, as in Proverbs 21:5: **"The plans of the diligent lead to profit, as surely as haste leads to poverty."**

The Globalist Party despised and mocked the Baros administration's accomplishments and achievements. For example, the year 2086 was clearly a boon for the United States and President

Baros's administration. The Winter Games were held in Alberta. Both United States hockey teams, men and women, earned gold. Furthermore, the United States dominated snowboarding and speed skating. The US beat out the rest of the countries, including Russia, for the most gold medals and total number of medals; this was the first year to include fourth- and fifth-place medals. The updated five-medal order was gold, silver, bronze, nickel, and copper. The scintillating and well-watched Winter Games were so successful that President Baros convinced the Winter Game Committee to hold the games in Alberta henceforth; the reasoning was to reduce the cost of building athletic stadiums and fields every four years. With the devoted assistance of the globalists, the media and agitprop indicated that none of these successes and others should be credited to President Baros. The media and globalists were fulfilling the words of President Gerald Ford: **"A coalition of groups is waging a massive propaganda campaign against the president of the United States. An all-out attack. Their aim is total victory for themselves and total defeat for him."**

Back at the beginning of 2088, the United States population was approximately 388 million, and the world had finally exceeded eight billion people again; however, the world population was projected to decline due to smaller families and a lower birthrate. Furthermore, the United States population was unchanged for over a decade. It took over forty years to recover from the events of the 2020 and 2030 decades; during both decades, a few billion people perished of famine from net-zero policy initiatives, adverse effects from vaccine shots and pandemics, as well as devastating wars; during the 2030 decade, more people succumbed from adverse effects of vaccines than any other cause except war. The vaccines had adverse effects since they manipulated and changed people's DNA, which destroyed their immune systems. Furthermore, the net-zero initiatives declared war on required resources like fertilizers and petroleum fuels, which resulted in less food production and drastically less heating during the winter. The relentless attacks on fossil fuels failed to heed American writer and philosopher Alex Epstein's axiom: **"The fact that oil is a "finite" material is not a problem...Every material is finite. Life is all about taking the theoretically finite but practically limitless materials in nature and creatively turning them into useful resources. The fossil fuel industry does it, the "renewable"—actually, the "unreliable"—energy industry doesn't. End of story."**

Governments that pushed the net-zero policies and initiatives failed to understand or did not care that the infrastructure took significantly longer than the goals stated. Thus, there was a significant increase in starvation and people freezing to death. Governments did not adhere to the wisdom of Alex Epstein: **"Net-zero policy, if actually implemented, would certainly be the most significant act of mass murder since the killings of one hundred million people by communist regimes in the twentieth century—and it would likely be far greater."**

Since October 2087, the world had dealt with another problematic Doggam pandemic similar to the eventual discovery of the 2020 and 2024 *plandemics;* however, the Doggam virus, thought to come from North Korea, was more contagious and deadlier than earlier viruses like COVID-19. COVID-19 affected the 2020 presidential election, since numerous states required mail-in voting that had questionable voter verification requirements. In the 2024 presidential election, a supposed bird flu epidemic occurred just in time to impact the election. However, the public opposed bird-flu lockdowns and mail-in voting, except in states controlled by globalists, which were referred to as "radical progressive states" at that time.

President Baros cautiously nominated Vice President Andrea Argento, assassinated Vice President Alfred Jones's replacement, knowing that the vox populi wanted him. Argento was the former Speaker of the House and had been in politics for eight years; most globalists loathed him. Both legislative houses, which at the time had a slim Nationalist-Party majority, confirmed the nomination. Soon after the confirmation, the House of Representatives flipped back to Globalist Party rule.

Vice President Andrea Argento was a seasoned prosecuting attorney in Tennessee for over twenty years before entering politics; additionally, he was the Tennessee Attorney General for two years. He had strong libertarian beliefs and was extremely patriotic. He completed ROTC and served four years in the army as a JAG officer. He was on active duty during the eighty-eight-day Venezuelan War; interestingly, President Baros and he served at the same air force base for over six months. Unfortunately, during the war, Andrea Argento lost his left arm in an enemy attack; fortunately, due to the advancement of technology, he had a bionic left arm that looked similar to a human arm. When they met, they discovered that their military careers had crossed paths on several occasions and they each knew several of the same people, such as Admiral Sarah Davis and Sergeant Major Kevin Nika; however, they had not met each other when they were serving. Comparable to President Baros, Argento had o his devoted high-school sweetheart and had six children. He and President Baros firmly believed in the wise words of George Orwell: **"The real division is not between conservatives and revolutionaries but between authoritarians and libertarians."** In addition, President Baros understood historian and philosopher Will Durant's axiom: **"Civilization begins with order, grows with liberty, and dies with chaos."** They both believed that to avoid civil chaos, we must accept personal responsibility for the nation's liberties. Both men understood Confucius's prudence: **"The virtuous man is driven by responsibility, the non-virtuous man is driven by profit."**

President Baros was a mechanical engineer and professional engineer from the great state of Indiana; he earned his master's degree in robotics; his bona fide professional passions were androids and space exploration. While he was in college, he completed ROTC and merited his commission as a second lieutenant; his beloved wife, Li Jing, graduated with him from the same university. Li Jing truly loved Marcus, and she was pleased that he was six-foot-two inches tall and physically fit; he had an Apollonian demeanor and was a bon vivant. She loved his gray hair and hazel eyes; she adored the fact that he regularly wore a suit and tie with a small United States Air Force flag pin on his suit lapel. He loyally served in the air force as a top-notch fighter pilot; he did eighteen combat mission flights and earned recognition as a flying ace for the number of enemy fighters that he shot down. His call name was Red Tiger; this was in honor of his Chinese wife's heritage, since he was born in the Chinese Year of the Tiger.

Li Jing, who spoke with a euphonious voice, was a petite, ravishing Chinese woman who regularly wore traditional red dresses with her pearl necklace. She adored her Chinese zodiac animal, a dragon. However, she adored Marcus even more. When she thought of Marcus, she fulfilled Lao Tzu's axiom of love: **"Being deeply loved by someone gives you strength, while loving someone deeply gives you courage."**

After four years, President Baros left the military as a captain soon after earning the Air Force Cross. His military service lived up to General Dwight D. Eisenhower's words: **"What counts is not necessarily the size of the dog in the fight—it's the size of the fight in the dog."**

After several years of fostering his estate and companies, Marcus Baros, with the support of Li Jing, became a multi-billionaire as a result of the enormous success of his Megadroid Company that his father started, and Marcus rocketed the organization to the next technological level; his father was also a mechanical engineer with a passion for creating and advancing robots. This successful worldwide megacompany created highly sophisticated robots and androids that could be used for labor from housework to the service industry. Furthermore, the Megadroid *fighterbots* were employed in the military, and the fighting *fighterbots* presently outnumbered the military service personnel almost two to one; the United States had more *fighterbots* than the rest of the world combined. Ironically, the United States' globalist-controlled states purchased and employed the Megadroid robots, since these remarkable robots were considered comparably inexpensive, dependable, sophisticated, upgradeable, and multifunctional; however, half the globalist-controlled states' robots were from Baros's competition. Baros tended to believe the words of Dennis Muilenberg, an American engineer: **"Robots allow our employees to work safely, faster, and at less cost."**

In addition, President Baros acquired the Maxploration Company, his other magnum opus, that led universally in space exploration, satellite launches, moon station management, and terraform operations on Mars, as well as the Martian station construction. Additionally, the military space force contracted with his effective megacorporation to build military satellites and launch them into orbit; these satellites had multiple uses, from being deadly weapons to communication or surveillance tools.

Due to the enormous success of his space conglomerate, the United States was the first country to send robots to Mars and the only country with a Martian station as well as spacelabs and satellites orbiting the planets from Mercury to Saturn. Currently, there were quarterly launches from the moon to Mars and monthly launches to the moon to operate the moon space station, and these stations were managed and constructed with Megadroid *spacebots*, sophisticated robots that are multifunctional and upgradeable. The moon station served other countries of the world, such as Russia and India. The moon station's primary purpose was to launch rockets into the rest of the solar system and observe the cosmos with an advanced telescope. The moon robots manned and maintained the moon station with the assistance of astronauts. The United States had a surreptitious moon station on the dark side of the moon, which was even more impressive.

Boros's megacompany oversaw the expansion of the space stations on both the moon and Mars. His organization advertised that the terraforming of Mars was expected to be complete in four to six years; currently, Mars had as much breathable air as there was on Mount Everest. In addition, near the equator of Mars, the temperature range was fifty to seventy degrees Fahrenheit. Maxploration Company continued—now on a limited basis—to operate laser technology to melt Martian land areas to create an atmosphere and release water from the depths of Mars. Furthermore, there were areas on Mars that could grow crops in a greenhouse and monthly rains in some locations. Maxploration Company developed *space-bot-operated spaceships* that traveled from Europa to Mars; these gigantic spaceships carried water from Europa, a moon of Jupiter, to Mars in order to create Martian seas and lakes. Thus, mankind should finally achieve Buzz Aldrin's vision: **"Going to Mars would evolve humankind into a two-planet species."**

The Maxploration and Megadroid companies adhered to Baros's philosophy of *TEAMS*. His corporations did not support Diversity, Equity, and Inclusion (DEI), which he advocated should DIE. President Baros believed that DEI emphasized judging people on immutable characteristics such as skin color and race, which were inherited and did not equate to any talent or merit; DEI was striving to punish individuals for unequal outcomes as well as actions of previous generations. His *TEAMS* acronym, which he explained during campaign speeches, stood for:

1. *Talent*: Organizations hire individuals because they possess the required skills. These individual talents and acumens are compensated based on supply and demand.

2. *Equality*: Everyone should be equal under the law and organizations' regulations.
3. *American*: Organizations and individuals should uphold the American Constitution and principles such as sovereign individual rights and liberty.
4. *Meritocracy*: individuals should be compensated for their merits and earnings, not their immutable traits; promotions should be awarded for an individual's proven advantages and skills.
5. *Synchronized*: For the organizational unit to succeed, members must believe in and understand the organization's purpose; individuals should seek organizations with which they can harmonize and ethically match. Both the organization and the individual must have the same teleological business aim.

President Baros and his family the words of Robert Reich, an American lawyer and professor: **"The liberal ideal is that everyone should have fair access and fair opportunity. This is not equality of result. It's equality of opportunity. There's a fundamental difference."** In addition, they understood the wisdom of David Samuel, Third Viscount Samuel, an Anglo-Israeli neurologist: **"Equality of opportunity is an equal opportunity to prove unequal talents."**

President Marcus Baros, with his lovely wife Li Jing, had six athletically and academically successful children during their marriage of over thirty-five years. Li Jing, with Marcus's support, was truly a prudent tiger mom who instilled discipline and passion for academic success in all her children. Their youngest daughter,

Teresa, and youngest son, Rex, attended Saint Peter Catholic High School, and their son Sean attended a private Catholic university. Sean was the tallest in the family at six foot eight; Rex was a stocky, muscular teenager at five foot ten. All the Baros men had dark black hair, except the president, who had some grey. Teresa was the youngest, a more petite version of her mother, with long black hair. Marcus joked with his beloved wife that Teresa was a mini Li Jing.

Sean, Theodore (who was called Father Theodore since he was a priest), and Walter were dedicated Eagle Scouts like their father, who was a former scoutmaster; Rex was still in Boy Scouts and working toward his Eagle rank. Nearly three years ago, before his eighteenth birthday, Sean earned his Eagle rank and double Silver Palm. His Eagle project was building a pedestrian rope bridge over a creek in a local school park next to Saint Peter Catholic High School. Troop 108, his family, friends, and Mariana, his longtime girlfriend, assisted in his project; Mariana was a bubbly, petite Hispanic college student with gorgeous long brunette hair. The pedestrian rope bridge with a wooden bridge deck took three weekends to construct.

Sean's journey in scouting began in Cub Scouts as a Tiger cub and crossed over to Boy Scouts. After completing Boy Scouts, he joined Venturing, since this was his forte; he did ten high adventures, including Philmont, as a Boy Scout and Venture Scout. Philmont is located in New Mexico and is one of the first high adventures in scouting. The older daughter, Lori, earned the Girl Scout Gold Award, the same as her current scout-leader mother; the younger daughter, Teresa, was still in Girl Scouts but had already earned her Silver Award. All had completed ten years of 4-H, except Teresa and Rex, who were still participating in 4-H. The Baros family adhered to the wisdom of Lord Robert Baden-Powell, founder of Boy Scouts: **"I have over and over again explained that the purpose of the Boy Scout and Girl Guide Movement is to build men and women as citizens endowed with the three H's, namely, Health, Happiness, and Helpfulness. The man or woman who succeeds in developing these three attributes has secured the main steps to success in this Life."**

President Baros's beloved wife, Li Jing, and he were high school sweethearts; Marcus and Li Jing were crowned their senior class homecoming couple. In addition, that same year, Marcus quarterbacked his football team to a second state championship in a row, and he was the catcher for his high school baseball team that lost in the state semifinals that same year. His beloved wife was the high school valedictorian and head cheerleader as well as a point guard; President Baros regularly teased her that she was the astute one in the family and the reason why the children had their excellent looks.

Since the youngest two children were still in high school outside the megalopolis area of Indianapolis, Li Jing stayed with them during the week in their mansion, and on the weekends they all went to the White House. Sean also attended a university in Indianapolis. Fortunately, the Baros family had a private jet called the *Baros Express* that could fly the family back and forth to the White House in Kansas. When the *Baros Express* flew as Air Force One, President Baros agreed with President George H. W. Bush: **"The thing I miss about Air Force One is they don't lose my luggage."**

Walter, the oldest son, was a dedicated defense lawyer; he was a younger version of President Baros in looks and mannerisms. He was just as athletic as his brothers and his father. He played sports in high school and college; he was comparable to Sean since he played both football and baseball. Interestingly, Sean was attending a 2A Catholic university with a football and baseball scholarship, which Walter had accomplished as well. Walter was an outstanding running back in both his alma maters; in his junior year, his college football team won the Division 2 national championship and he broke his college rushing record. He still enjoyed playing tennis with his loving wife, Julia. Walter respected George Orwell's adage: **"Threats to freedom of speech, writing, and action, though often trivial in isolation, are cumulative in their effect and, unless checked, lead to a general disrespect for the rights of the citizen."**

Lori, their precious older daughter, was also a defense attorney akin to her brother Walter and practiced law with him at the same law firm. She and her younger sister, Teresa, resembled her mother; however, she was exceptionally tall at six feet. She was just as athletic and academic as her brothers. She was a successful volleyball player at both her high school and college; her college team won a national championship in her junior year. Two years ago, Lori and her husband, John, were married by her brother, Father Theodore. Lori and her brother Theodore had an exceptional brother-sister bond and were very respectful.

Father Theodore was by far the best baseball player in the family. He was a pitcher for his Catholic university baseball team, which won two national college championships. Father Theodore could have been a professional baseball player; however, he refused the offer so that he could be a priest and teacher; he taught at Saint Peter Catholic High School. Father Theodore desired to serve Jesus, like Peter in Mathew 16:18: **"And I say also unto thee, That thou art Peter, and upon this rock I will build my church; and the gates of hell shall not prevail against it."**

President Baros and his wife, Li Jing, were criticized by the globalists and secular media for Baros's devout Christian beliefs and traditional family values. Li Jing was well-known for quoting John 3:16: **"For God so loved the world, that he gave his only begotten Son, that whosoever believeth in him should not perish, but have everlasting life."** In addition, with their second oldest son Theodore being an ordained Catholic priest, the media, who were self-identified cosmopolitans, tended to express that the first family were fanatical Christian fundamentalists. This was clearly exaggerated; the press (the unelected fourth estate) ridiculed the Baros family for believing that rights come from God and not from the government. Furthermore, the president's seemingly deep commitment to free market economic principles and limited government was constantly under relentless attacks by the legacy media. When the media attacks became caustic and ad hominem, Li Jing would remind her family of the wise words of George Orwell: **"The further a society drifts from truth, the more it will hate those who speak it."** Furthermore, she optimistically expressed that God would win in the end. She regularly reminded all of 2 Corinthians 2:14: **"Now thanks be unto God, which always causeth us to triumph in Christ, and maketh manifest the savor of his knowledge by us in every place."**

Prior to running for president, President Baros had never held any political office. Early in his life, the media gave him relatively positive press due to the great success of his organizations; however, that all drastically changed when he entered the political fray as a presidential candidate. He deeply understood the words of Italy's President Sergio Mattarella: **"I had no intention of entering politics, but then the force of events led me to become involved in politics."**

In the brutal 2084 election, the presidential candidate Marcus Baros exhibited his extremely populist and America-first patriotic style; he surprisingly beat a deep-state-supported globalist candidate, Congressman Dillon Drakos, who was heavily funded by *Mr. Black Rose*, secretly known by only a few and a staunch supporter of globalist politicians and causes. President-Elect Baros won the electoral college decisively 578 to 400; however, he lost the popular vote by a couple of million; if you hypothetically did not include the largest globalist-controlled state, California, then President-Elect Baros won the popular vote by three million. The electoral college had increased extensively in numbers over the years due to the addition of the *three senators per state amendment* and *a congressperson per half-million persons amendment*, as well as a significantly increased American population. His unexpected victory clearly was a surprise to the Globalist Party and the global elites; the 2084 election was an unpredictable black swan event for the deep state and globalists, who were convinced that nationalist control would be a *1984* Orwellian nightmare. *Mr. Black Rose* was disappointed with the results. Furthermore, the previous globalist-controlled administration spied and eavesdropped on President Baros's incoming administration; the deep state was clearly not willing to cooperate with his administration as well. After being spied on, President Baros quickly learned from

George Orwell's wise words: **"If you want to keep a secret, you must also hide it from yourself."**

Congressman Drakos, a devout Marxist globalist, was on his sixth term for the great state of New York; ironically, he was constitutionally required to sit out twelve years. He advocated for secular globalutopianism, a global world order that guarantees a utopian society for all, without religion. *Globalutopianism* was a neologism created soon after the rise of the national and globalist parties. He was one of the few people in ***Mr. Black Rose's*** inner circle. Congressman Drakos adamantly disagreed with Rush Limbaugh, an American political commentator: **"Capitalism is always evaluated against dreams. Utopia is a dream. It doesn't exist."**

During those non-congressional years as a DC lobbyist, Congressman Drakos clearly was taken care of. Suspiciously, he economically prospered significantly during his lobbyist periods; this was still a societal illness that plagued the political process. He lobbied for secular globalutopianist causes. Before being a US congressman, he was a New York State congressman for three terms; Congressman Drakos, well-known for speaking with circumlocution, had been a shady elected official or lobbyist since graduating from a prestigious elite law school. He was a devout disciple of the Globalist Party with an almost religious fervor; he had a very uncouth, egocentric demeanor. He desired to be a despot in order to fulfill his iconoclastic vision; he despised traditionalism, conservatism, and traditional religion of any kind. Politically, he thought that it was ultimately futile to work with the nationalists. He regularly expressed the following quote from Karl Marx: **"Taxes are the source of life for the bureaucracy,** the army, and the court, in short, for the whole apparatus of the executive power. Strong government and heavy taxes are identical."

Congressman Drakos querulously advocated for the overwhelming expansion of the federal government and drastically limiting the states' rights. He secretly wanted to get rid of the states. Congressman Drakos abhorred the federal republic form of government; he wanted to depose the American way of life. He promoted raising taxes radically on the top 5 percent of earners to pay their fair share. This sounds like a good idea; however, the top 5 percent could easily pass their cost on to others, like the poor and middle class, which would adversely affect them. Thus, excessive taxing inevitably adversely affects the working class. The globalists' governmental obsession adhered to James Madison's words: **"The power of taxing people and their property is essential to the very existence of government."**

President Baros easily won the Nationalist Party's presidential nomination; however, he realized that he had the Nationalist Party's sword of Damocles over his head since he did not unquestionably toe the party's deep-state line. The president shared Alexander Hamilton's skepticism: **"Nothing could be more ill-judged than that intolerant spirit which has, at all times, characterized political parties."**

Coincidentally, in June of 2088, a politically globalist-controlled city, Progressiveville, in California, filed a civil suit against the Baros family. The four-billion-dollar lawsuit claimed that the Megadroid Company was liable for the assassin robot's actions during Memorial Day in DC, Kansas; Walter was in control of both of the families' mega-corporations, Megadroid and

Maxploration, while his father served as president. Megadroid had one of its major *servicebot* and *fighterbot* manufacturing plants in Progressiveville. The infamous goal was to bankrupt the organization and hold the Baros family liable. In addition, this also served to interfere with President Baros's campaign schedule, similar to how opponents interfered with President Trump in the 2024 election. The naive globalists did not consider the company and robots' popularity, or they did not care about the economic and social ramifications. The enormously successful company employed nearly half the city's workforce in well-paying occupations and careers. If the successful Megadroid Company relocated or declared bankruptcy, the city would collapse and die economically. The concerned citizens of Progressiveville encouraged others to hold peaceful and lawful protests. Their message emphasized the importance of their jobs and livelihood as they relied on the Megadroid Company. However, the globalists had plans to prevent any demonstrations from countering their agenda. Hence, when the protests occurred, numerous protestors were arrested by *policebots* with shoot-to-kill orders for anyone resisting arrest or not dispersing when ordered to do so. Progressiveville authorities adhered to George Orwell's words regarding the police state: **"Big Brother is watching you."**

In Progressiveville alone, eight protesters were murdered and hundreds were arrested and injured. The legacy media blamed the protesting on the president. The legacy media failed to understand that the alternate social media were able to divulge the complete story and let the world know that the globalists were willing to violate citizens' right to peaceful protest. Besides, in all globalist-controlled states, the highly unpopular *policebots* were not accountable and had sovereign immunity from civil liability for shooting or decimating citizens, regardless of the circumstances. The authority became the sovereign's whim of Voltaire's warning: **"The sovereign is called a tyrant who knows no laws but his caprice."**

2.

THE TRIAL AND IMPEACHMENT

REX, BAROS'S YOUNGEST SON, was the catcher for his team at the Saint Peter 3A regional baseball championship in early June of 2088; Father Theodore coached him to be an exceptional catcher. Father Theodore could not convince Rex to be a pitcher even though he had a wicked throw. He hit one home run with two runners on base and hit three for four for the game; he was the best batter on the team with a .358 batting average and led the team with home runs. The game went into extra innings. Unfortunately, the Saint Peter Golden Knights lost by a walk-off solo home run. The team ended its season with a 23–5 record. Rex was inspired by MLB catcher Bill Dickey's words: **"A catcher must want to catch. He must make up his mind that it isn't the terrible job it is painted, and that he isn't going to say every day, 'Why, oh why with so many other positions in baseball did I take up this one.'"**

Rex, in his coming senior year, would play lacrosse, football, and disk golf for Saint Peter Catholic High School; last May, Rex's lacrosse team lost in the regional championship, in which he played goalie. Rex concurred with Jim Brown, NFL and lacrosse player: **"I'd rather play lacrosse six days a week and football on the seventh."**

During the Division 2 college regional games in early June, Sean, a southpaw, was pitching for Saint Daniel Catholic University in Indianapolis. He pitched a two-hitter and three-walk game; he also went three for four in hitting and drove in one run with an impressive double. In this first game in the morning, they were victorious, winning 3–1. Unfortunately, that evening, the Saint Daniel Roaring Lions lost to the team that eventually became the Division 2 national champions.

Father Theodore, who coached and taught Sean how to pitch, was at the games. He was very proud of his brother's performance in sports and academics in his junior year; he had high optimism that Sean would have an incredible senior year. Father Theodore agreed with baseball legend Babe Ruth's words: **"Baseball was, is, and always will be the best game in the world to me."**

The following week, in June of 2088, Father Theodore went to visit his sister Teresa in the semi-state girls' softball game. Father Theodore taught Teresa to pitch as well; however, Teresa threw the softball with her right hand and threw it with an impressive spin. (Father Theodore, a Jesuit priest, taught mathematics and physics at Saint Peter Catholic High School; he tutored his younger siblings in mathematics and physics, which inspired Sean to be an engineer. Unfortunately, all three—Rex, Teresa, and Sean—had Father Theodore as their math or physics teacher.) Teresa threw a no-hitter until the seventh inning; however, the one hit was not a threat. The Saint Peter Golden Knights softball team won 3–0.

Father Theodore was extremely proud of his sister and was looking forward to the state championship game. After the game, Teresa asked her brother to give her some advice since she struck out three times. Father reminded her of Babe Ruth's words: **"Never let the fear of striking out keep you from playing the game."** Unfortunately, the girls' softball team lost in the state championship and ended up with an outstanding record of 25–3.

Sofia, Teresa's best friend, and Teresa enjoyed the rest of the summer before going back to school as juniors. The two friends were petite young girls heading into their junior year. Lori regularly joked that they were sisters from different mothers. Teresa and Sofia exemplified Aristotle's adage: **"What is a friend? A single soul dwelling in two bodies."**

The Baros family dined together at the White House the day before Independence Day 2088. Butler Charles, who was like a member of the family, was assisted by his *servicebot* staff and prepared a savory, appetizing meal of ribeye steak and potatoes. His dress and actions exemplified a stereotypical professional butler since he went to a prestigious culinary school. Butler Charles oversaw eight *servicebots*, four of which he called by their functions: *Chauffeur, Educator, Maid,* and *Cook*; the other four *servicebots* assisted the primary four. Butler Charles and Chef Rosa had been members of the Baros staff for over twenty-seven years and the only humans who worked at the Baros estate; all the other servants and staff were robots. In addition, Butler Charles and Rosa had been married to each other for over twenty-five years. Rosa had exceptional culinary skills. She and Charles were devoted servants who enjoyed being part of the Baros extended family. They had a daughter in college, and Baros had given her a full-ride scholarship for her nursing degree. In the early years, they acted in loco parentis for all the Baros children.

The Baros family congratulated Teresa, Rex, and Sean on their superior performance in their respective team sports. In addition, all three had straight As and were on the honor roll. Sean reminded all that Mariana was on the dean's list again for nursing. The Baros family discussed their plans for the Fourth of

July event tomorrow. President Baros expressed the importance of security since the entire immediate family would be there.

At the White House the next day, President Baros presented an excellent speech prior to the resplendent fireworks and spectacular drone light show, which was choreographed with patriotic music and included enormous holographs depicting historical events and persons. His speech emphasized the success of the United States and its remarkable history; he included that the United States possessed the world's oldest successful constitution, even though some had strived to destroy our way of life in the 2020s. The event ended with fighter jets screeching over the White House and audience, releasing red, white, and blue smoke. President Baros's speech included the words of Theodore Roosevelt: **"Americanism means the virtues of courage, honor, justice, truth, sincerity, and hardihood—the virtues that made America."**

A couple of days after Independence , Lori, with her dedicated team of lawyers, was in a grandiose Progressiveville, California, courtroom while the rest of the citizens lived in an impoverished and crime-infested state; Lori was there to defend her dad. The recently passed California law, which may not have been constitutional, proclaimed that all courts under this law would not be authorized to have a jury. Judge Richard Pilot, a globalist-elected judge, adamantly agreed with the DA Jerome Williams and declare a summary judgment of liability and fraudulent product. This judgment was a consequence of violating a recently passed, untested, and previously unenforced California law; this law read that an organization was liable for their products even when someone else used their product in a crime; the globalist-controlled legislative branch specifically passed this law to take down the president and his companies. The globalist DA Jerome Williams had been elected two years ago; he campaigned to ruin President Baros and his corrupt business. DA Williams regularly stated that President Baros should lose his assets, spend the rest of his life in prison, and be destitute.

During his campaigns, Jerome Williams expressed, "President Baros is not our president. He is a criminal and tyrant." Of course, DA Jerome Williams's entire campaign disregarded the crime, violence, and depravity within his city; his campaign was funded secretly by the mysterious *Mr. Black Rose*; he was one of the hidden benefactors of a cabal that very few knew existed, and his trusted lieutenants would eliminate anyone who revealed anything about him. Ironically, DA Williams never met *Mr. Black Rose*; however, DA Williams received all of *Mr. Black Rose's* directives through Congressman Drakos. Progressiveville had the highest per capita crime rate in the country; paradoxically, the Megadroid Company grounds were well-secured and had practically no crime. DA Jerome Williams adhered to Karl Marx's objective: **"My object in life is to dethrone God and destroy capitalism."**

The defense argued adamantly that their client was not given an opportunity to defend himself. The defense argued that the president's constitutional rights were violated, such as the Seventh Amendment: **"In suits at common law, where the value in controversy shall exceed twenty dollars, the right of trial by jury shall be preserved, and no fact tried by a jury, shall be otherwise reexamined in any court of the United States, than according to the rules of the common law."** This amendment was violated since the president was denied a trial by jury.

In addition, this recently passed law did specify immunity if the product was tampered with. The arrogant judge deemed that this civil court would continue in order to determine damages; however, within the next thirty days, the Megadroid Company must be liquified as a corporation.

Lori's team immediately filed an appeal. Within days, the appellate court placed a stay on dissolving Baros's business until damages were determined and appeals were exhausted. The appellate court understood the sentiment of Finlet Peter Dunne, an American journalist: **"An appeal is when you ask one court to show its contempt for another court."**

Outside the courtroom, during a press conference, Lori expressed, "This is a complete tragedy of justice. We have not been given an opportunity to defend ourselves. This is an untested and unconstitutional law, since the law denies the defense to have a jury trial. A politically elected judge with an axe to grind determined liability without the defense presenting any evidence. We are experiencing the use of lawfare against the president and his family, similar to the historical 2024 presidential trials and events; the 2024 lawfare resulted in dividing the country and distrust of the legal system. Besides, this verdict adversely affects the lives of over thirty thousand Megadroid employees and their families. As you are aware, we have won our appeal to at least prevent the dissolving of Megadroid for now. However, the judge has placed a gag order on the president and his lawyers, which limits what we can say. This gag order is clearly unconstitutional."

DA Jerome Williams, the State's plaintiff attorney, had two witnesses testify at the California civil court. The first witness testified that the three *model P-46 fighterbots* were built and manufactured by the Megadroid Company. During cross-examination, the witness confirmed that the *P-46* robots were reprogrammed and that the assassination did not occur in California; thus, *P-46* robots were deliberately tampered with. The plaintiff's witness confirmed that the unlawful act occurred in DC, Kansas, which is clearly out of California's jurisdiction. The plaintiff's lawyer objected that the witness was not an expert in regard to where the unlawful event occurred.

The defense responded to the plaintiff, DA Williams, with the obvious question, "Is there a plaintiff expert witness that could verify a crime by any Megadroid *P-46* robots within California?"

The plaintiff had no expert witness to verify this. The second witness attested basically the same as the first, except with a more technical explanation. The second witness revealed, through highly technical evidence, that the initial installed programming clearly had been altered; this alteration guaranteed the transformation of the original *P-46* robots into three assassins without any safeguards. The defense immediately requested a dismissal since this court and case did not have jurisdiction. The judge denied their request. Obviously, the defense team appealed the judge's decision.

At the California trial, Lori's legal defense team went on the offense; simultaneously, peaceful protestors were protesting outside of the courthouse for the Baros family. The legal dream team had an expert witness thoroughly explain the well-developed safety protocols of Megadroid Company; these safety protocols ensured the safety of the *P-46* robots if not tampered with. This famous legal expert explained that this court did not have jurisdiction, since the altered *P-46* robots did their acts in another state.

Furthermore, all individuals who were harmed or murdered were not California citizens; this included the security guards. Another well-known legal expert explained that California law exempted product liability if the item was tampered with or altered, which had been established. As both sides rested their case, the judge was ready to declare his verdict. Judge Richard Pilot knew that he had a plethora of laws to choose from. He disagreed with the wisdom of Tacitus, a Roman Historian: **"The more corrupt the state, the more numerous the laws."**

Judge Richard Pilot decisively declared that Megadroid was liable and owed four billion dollars in punitive damages. He recognized that this judgment would be appealed, and the appellate court placed a stay on liquidating the Megadroid Company until appeals were exhausted. The next day, Lori's legal team immediately appealed the dubious decision. Simultaneously, several state senators and congressmen filed ethics violations against Judge Richard Pilot and DA Jerome Williams; their obvious ethical complaints were that this court had no jurisdiction and the case was purely politically motivated; furthermore, even if the court had jurisdiction, the court ignored the law's explicit exemption if the product was tampered with.

President Baros was meeting with his legal team. The lawyers in the California trial stated that if they did not win on appeal, they would immediately appeal to the California Supreme Court; however, the president was required by the judge to secure a four-billion-dollar bond before appealing; fortunately, the appellate court thought the bond was excessive and reduced it to one billion. The lawyers argued that this excessive bond was in violation of the Eighth Amendment: **"Excessive bail shall not be required, nor excessive fines imposed, nor cruel and unusual punishments inflicted."** The lawyer stated that the president's right to due process was violated, which is in Section One of the Fourteenth Amendment: **"All persons born or naturalized in the United States, and subject to the jurisdiction thereof, are citizens of the United States and the State wherein they reside. No State shall make or enforce any law which shall abridge the privileges or immunities of citizens of the United States; nor shall any State deprive any person of life, liberty, or property, without due process of law; nor deny to any person within its jurisdiction the equal protection of the laws."** He also mentioned the Fifth Amendment: **"...nor shall be compelled in any criminal case to be a witness against himself, nor be deprived of life, liberty, or property, without due process of law; nor shall private property be taken for public use, without just compensation."**

Interestingly, the president agreed to fund the one-billion-dollar reduced bond, which he, fortunately, had liquidated funds for; he believed that this would accelerate the process and the appeal and prevent DA Jerome Williams from seizing his businesses and assets, which the DA was threatening to execute. Besides, a billion dollars in 2088 was worth approximately a hundred million dollars in 2020. As a result of tenfold inflation, the current highbrow lexicon established the following neologisms in America: *decamillionaire, hectomillionaire, decabillionaire,* and *hectobillionaire.*

These, respectively, were equivalent to possessing the following net worth: ten million dollars, one hundred million dollars, ten billion dollars, and one hundred billion dollars. In 2088, a few individuals and families had become trillionaires. The globalists still believed in inflation and adhered to the sentiment of Russian Marxist Vladimir Lenin: **"The way to crush the bourgeoisie is to grind them between the millstones of taxation and inflation."**

On a gorgeous, tranquil summer day in August 2088, President Baros was convening with his dedicated cabinet. President Baros inquisitively stated, "The House of Representatives and Senate have sent us another bloated foreign-aid bill to my desk that directs, of course, that hundreds of billions of dollars would be allocated to another endless war between Marxist Nicaragua and Costa Rica. As expected, the bill does not direct or verify where or how the money is allocated. I shall veto this worthless, inflated bill. We have our own domestic problems, and we should not overburden the taxpayers. Besides, these two nations' antipathy toward each other must end; we cannot just send money all the time without any acceptable resolution. The taxpayers deserve a good return on their investments." President Baros agreed with the attitude of Walter E. Williams's statement: **"Conservatives and liberals are kindred spirits as far as government spending is concerned. First, let's make sure we understand what government spending is. Since government has no resources of its own, and since there's no Tooth Fairy handing Congress the funds for the programs it enacts, we are forced to recognize that government spending is no less than the confiscation of one person's property to give it to another to whom it does not belong—in effect, legalized theft."**

President Baros adamantly opposed endless wars, which were funded by the working class and the blood of young soldiers. He understood that the military-industrial complex favored endless wars in order to make money from the taxpayers. President Baros firmly understood the words of George Orwell: **"The war is not meant to be won; it is meant to be continuous. A hierarchical society is only possible on the basis of poverty and ignorance. This new version is the past, and no different past can ever have existed. In principle, the war effort is always planned to keep society on the brink of starvation. The war is waged by the ruling group against its own subjects and its object is not the victory over either Eurasia or East Asia, but to keep the very structure of society intact."** Furthermore, President Baros was not a pacifist; however, he wanted to limit the military-industrial complex and disagreed with the war hawks and deep state war efforts. President Baros understood American political activist Ralph Nader's warning: **"President Eisenhower warned us, five-star general, he said watch out for the military-industrial complex. That's a threat to our freedom, to our economy, and what we have now is a gigantic taxpayer draining empire that is devouring itself, which, as you say, it's creating more resistance, more fighting, against us overseas."**

President Baros carefully listened to his cabinet's recommendations on how to end the war, as well as reasons to send resources, money, or aid to Costa Rica. Unfortunately, his cabinet was not aware that Nicaragua globalists were funded and supported by *Mr. Black Rose* and the cabal in order to expand the globalists' influence into Costa Rica. The President steadfastly insisted that the recommendation must include an end state and metrics that revealed success or failure; he explained that we must understand that everything should not be on the backs of the United States taxpayers. President Baros reminded his cabinet of lessons from Ronald Reagan's quote: **"We don't have a trillion-dollar debt because we haven't taxed enough; we have a trillion-dollar debt because we spend too much."**

Ironically, the judicious California appellate court completed their review of the case; the appellate judges were nationalist-appointed judges; fortunately, a few years ago, a one-term nationalist governor had appointed numerous judges. The appellate court overturned the trial court's decision on several grounds. First, the court did not have jurisdiction, since all victims resided in another state, even though the product, *P-46*, had been manufactured in California. Second, even if the lower court had jurisdiction and the product had been used in a crime in California, then the fact that the product, *P-46*, had been drastically tampered with was evidence to prevent product liability. Third, the lower court, without a doubt, did not demonstrate adequate evidence for a summary judgment that concluded that the defendant was fraudulent; this was obviously in error or judicial derogatory bias against the defendant based on the lack of evidence presented before summary judgment. This questionable summary judgment seemed to be based only on mere accusations without proof. The appellate court concluded that Megadroid Company was not liable and would not be required to pay any damages; furthermore, due to the reckless nature of the lower court, the appellate court required that the lower court pay for all legal fees of the defendant and punitive damages of ten million dollars. The DA, Jerome Williams, immediately appealed the aforementioned decision. The California Supreme Court responded with a concurrence of the appellate court. The California Supreme Court reassured the intent of Alexander Hamilton's declaration: **"I think the first duty of society is justice."**

President Baros was pleased with the appellate court's decision. He instructed his legal team to donate ten million dollars and an additional ten million dollars of his money to assist the victims of the Memorial Day event. At a press conference he stated, "I truly believe that the appellate court got it right. Unfortunately, we should not celebrate until the murderers are placed behind bars. There were hundreds of persons slain, and numerous were injured that day by a reprogrammed robot that an evil person had tampered with. The *P-46* is comparable to a sword in Lucius Annaeus Seneca's words: **'A sword never kills anybody; it is a tool in the killer's hand.'** We must hold the criminals accountable for their evil acts."

The legacy media were absolutely shocked by the appellate court's decision to reverse the lower court; they immediately proclaimed that this was the worst legal decision that they had ever witnessed. The enraged media claimed that the appellate court did not recognize the magnitude of the damages and loss of life caused by the three Megadroid *P-46* robots regardless of their location and whether they had been tampered with; the biased appellate court did not consider that the three *P-46* robots were designed to neutralize, which was why the military had them. Moreover, the furious media expressed that the appellate court did not consider sovereign immunity, even if one agreed that the lower court was in error. Furthermore, the media cried that Baros should donate more than just twenty million dollars to the murdered individuals' families. The media adamantly advocated the words of union leader Richard Trumka: **"Friends, I'm angry about what's happening in politics today! Why is it wrong to ask the wealthiest people and most profitable corporations to pay their fair share?"** Next, the livid media had another complete meltdown when the California Supreme Court upheld the appellate court's decision. The media asserted that the California Supreme Court judges were just nationalist activists and were corrupt. The legacy media tended to agree with Nazi propagandist Joseph Goebbels: **"If you repeat a lie often enough, people will believe it, and you will even come to believe it yourself."**

In September of 2088, President Baros was on a worldwide live feed for the inauguration of the first operational space elevator. The impressive Maxploration *Alpha-Omega space elevator* ran from the South Pole of Antarctica to a space lab. This scientifically advanced elevator was sixty-five thousand miles long, nearly a fourth of the way to the moon. The technological marvel was connected to a stupendous space lab with an advanced telescope. It took over eight hours to travel from the South Pole to the space lab; however, the elevator was spacious with several comfort amenities such as a console and kitchenette; it could accommodate six astronauts comfortably; in addition, there were two lifts in order to allow one ascending and the other descending; each lift had its respective tube, and both tubes were connected. The outer sixty-five-thousand-mile elevator shaft was well-lit with warning lights to prevent aircraft and spaceships from hitting the elevator. The *Alpha-Omega space lab*, with a white interior, was capable of comfortably housing eight astronauts; interestingly, as the Earth rotated, the space lab could fix its position or allow the Earth to rotate the lab in twenty-four hours. Furthermore, in the future, the space lab would be expandable using augmented space pods. The *Alpha-Omega space lab* had enough lights and size to be detected by the naked eye at night from the South Pole.

Commander Brian Baru stated, "Mr. President, the view is breathtaking and inspiring. The space lab's operations are a complete go; our mission will be a complete success." The commander reminded the world of Edwin Powell Hubble's words: **"Equipped with our five senses—along with telescopes and microscopes and mass spectrometers and seismographs and magnetometers and particle accelerators and detectors sensitive to the entire electromagnetic spectrum—we explore the universe around us and call the adventure science."**

For promotional reasons at the *Alpha-Omega space lab*, Commander Brian Baru, a chess grandmaster, was willing to play a chess match against Russian grandmaster Petrov. The match was televised internationally, which gave the space lab and program international notoriety; the chess match would be played with a magnetic chess set to avoid gravitational problems; the chess pieces were either gold or silver. Of course, the astronauts explained the benefits of the space program and the space lab while Commander Brian Baru and Grandmaster Petrov played chess. They mentioned some additional galaxies and Earth-like planets, habitable exoplanets that were millions of light-years away. Commander Brian Baru won both games, resulting in a United States citizen being the first World Chess Champion since 2048.

Commander Brian Baru was the youngest astronaut and an astrophysics prodigy who had married his college sweetheart just before this mission; she referred to him as her devoted wunderkind. His lovely bride was also an astronaut. The baby-faced commander was a disciple of chess grandmaster Bobby Fischer, who said: **"Chess is a war over the board. The object is to crush the opponent's mind."**

In September of 2088, President Baros negotiated a ceasefire between the belligerent Nicaragua and overwhelmed Costa Rica. These countries agreed to the terms of the truce for the next six months in order to discuss ways to resolve their border disputes and other concerns. Currently, numerous Nicaraguans were illegally immigrating to Costa Rica through an unprotected border. Over 30 percent of the population within Costa Rica were former Nicaraguans. Moreover, a significant number of Nicaraguans within Costa Rica were part of the Marxist rebels attempting to overthrow the Costa Rican government. Nicaragua was clearly a tyrannical Marxist country and a globalist elite stronghold; *Mr. Black Rose* and the cabal were suspected of funding the Marxist Nicaraguans. The globalist elites controlled approximately 40 percent of world governments; of course, China, Iran, Iraq, Sudan, and North Korea were still their model tyrannical countries; these countries were committing numerous human rights violations and were notorious for committing democide; these governmental murders included politicide and outright killings for population control. These tyrannical nations validated George Orwell's warning: **"All tyrannies rule through fraud and force, but once the fraud is exposed, they must rely exclusively on force."**

The Costa Rican government strived to remain a democratic representative republic with human rights and a constitution. President Baros negotiated a ceasefire; Nicaragua would prevent its citizens from immigrating to Costa Rica for at least two years, and the United States promised to send necessary medical supplies and food to both countries; however, no transfer of funds would be granted. President Baros concurred with President John F. Kennedy: **"Let us never negotiate out of fear. But let us never fear to negotiate."**

At a packed Indianapolis campaign rally in an indoor football stadium, President Baros stated, "My hidden, mundane, and surreptitious opponent, Senator Cain, refuses to debate me and prefers to hide in his basement. Furthermore, his candidate for vice president, Carl Flight, refuses to debate my running mate, Andrea Argento. Carl Flight is a devoted Marxist and globalist; ironically, he is also a multibillionaire who made his money from capitalism. In addition, the globalist party prefers to play politics with lawfare, like the California trial. Senator Cain's entire campaign was a campaign of fear and avoidance; he believed that the expansion of government was the solution to everything, and he disdained free markets and liberty. As a result of the Doggam pandemic, he wants to lock down the entire country. The United States is the home of the free and the brave; we are not the home of the enslaved and the spineless." President Baros believed that most globalists, such as Senator Cain, Carl Flight, and Congressman Drakos, secretly adhered to the words of Nazi Heinrich Himmler: **"The best political weapon is the weapon of terror. Cruelty commands respect. Men may hate us. But, we don't ask for their love, only for their fear."**

The popular nationalist candidate, President Baros, was seeking his reelection. His well-attended campaigns were based on his extraordinary success during his first term; he succeeded in reducing governmental red tape and lowering taxes on the middle class. He concurred with Ronald Reagan's sentiment: **"Government's view of the economy could be summed up in a few short phrases: If it moves, tax it. If it keeps moving, regulate it. And if it stops moving, subsidize it."** His remarkable accomplishments included keeping the country out of endless wars and conflicts.

President Baros promoted staying out of the internal conflict between the separatists and the Argentina government; these tensions had significantly amplified ever since Argentina discovered a gigantic untapped lithium mine. President Baros believed in the prudence of Sun Tzu's axiom: **"There is no instance of a nation benefiting from prolonged warfare."** Many in Congress wanted military involvement, especially the globalists that were under the control of *Mr. Black Rose*, which the President warned could result in expanding the war or potentially leading to another world war. *Mr. Black Rose* wanted Argentina to be a globalist-controlled nation due to their rich resources like lithium. President Baros reminded all of the wise words of Dwight D. Eisenhower: **"The only way to win World War III is to prevent it."** Currently, Argentina was controlled by the nationalists as a result of failed socialist governments before 2024. Argentina continued to reform under the leadership of President Javier Milei's, who said: **"Socialists don't like the invisible hand; they prefer the claws of the state."**

President Baros negotiated several impressive peace deals and treaties. For example, he successfully negotiated an equitable truce between the young nations of Quebec and Ontario, which resulted in increased commerce and trade between the two young nations; the tension was over water rights, and Ontario was split between globalist and nationalist control. President Baros strongly believed in Abraham Lincoln's saying: **"Do I not destroy my enemies when I make them my friends?"**

During President Baros's first term, the country experienced an exceptional economy. This economic achievement significantly improved the standard of living for the middle and working class without any increased taxes or inflation; furthermore, food and energy prices were at a fifty-year low and significantly decreased during his presidency. Since the United States had over half the world's gold and silver, the president leveraged this fact with the rest of the world. This resulted in the US dollar being the global currency. At many of President Baros's campaign rallies, he advocated for the continuance of gold-backed currency based on the prudent saying of President Herbert Hoover: **"We have gold because we cannot trust governments."**

He signed and campaigned for a comprehensive energy bill called *Energy Independence,* which led to the country being more energy-autonomous. This comprehensive bill encouraged and financed the building of forty-five nuclear power plants and the implementation of numerous hydroelectric tidal generators. The proposed nuclear plants were technologically improved, and each one could service over twenty million persons; moreover, the disposal of nuclear waste had exponentially advanced. Furthermore, the bill increased the expansion of the Alberta pipeline to key refineries in the United States; it upgraded and expanded the Alberta pipeline that replaced the sabotaged pipeline, for which the rebel globalists were the suspected saboteurs. This bill modernized the energy grid with Tesla energy towers to secure energy for every citizen. The Tesla energy expansion practically resulted in extremely inexpensive energy. Realistically, energy poverty existed only in globalist-controlled states. The country was utterly energy independent and the world leader in exporting energy. President Baros explained to his staff that they should adhere to the wisdom of Herman Cain: **"The one thing that the President can do is to establish a real energy independence plan. We have all the resources we need right here in this country to establish energy independence if we had the leadership."**

In addition, the superpower United States was enjoying the expansion of advanced innovations such as inexpensive and practical hydro-cars and autonomous vehicles; these cars were propelled by converting water into oxygen and hydrogen; thus, the hydro-cars exhausted oxygen and were fueled by hydrogen. In addition, a successful corporation, Airborne Autocraft, manufactured practical and affordable hovercrafts such as the models *DT45* and *DT47*, which were also hydro-vehicles; these hovercrafts reduced the wear and tear on highways. Furthermore, the expanded trucking industry was over 70 percent autonomous vehicles. For safety reasons and reduced congestion, the trucking enterprise was encouraged to transport at night, incentivized by tax cuts. In addition, autonomous high-speed trains connected over 90 percent of cities with at least half a million people or more. The country was enjoying increased crop yields with minimal adverse environmental effects. Exact-Farm Equipment, a professional brand name, manufactured systematic computerized agricultural equipment that monitored a plant's life cycle. This exceptional equipment safeguarded that plants received the precise amount of fertilizer and water as well as weed and insect control; moreover, this reduced the overuse of hazardous insecticides and herbicides. The United States became the premier breadbasket of the world again. One of President Baros's notable administrative achievements in 2085 was the acquisition of Greenland from Denmark, expanding the country's territory. The critics called this the *Baros Frozen Folly*, claiming that the Greenland acquisition was a total waste of money with outrageous future liabilities. Soon after the purchase from the Scandinavian Federal Republic, rare earth elements (REEs) were discovered, such as nickel, lithium, and uranium; furthermore, additional diamond, silver, and coal mines were found and unearthed. These discoveries quieted the critics; furthermore, there were hundreds of thousands of Americans moving to Greenland for the get-rich *Greenland 2086ers Silver Rush*. The Silver Rush was a significant economic boon for Greenland, leading to rapid expansion. The success in Greenland inspired Greece to seek to become part of the United States in order to improve its economic situation. Currently, there are petitions from both Greenland and Greece to become the sixty-third and sixty-fourth states of the United States. Unfortunately, globalist rebels attempted to sabotage a cluster of Greenland silver mines with a dirty nuke; fortunately, the military foiled their treacherous plans prior to detonation. After a Navy SEAL disarmed the dirty nuke, he found several *black roses*; fortunately, he did not touch any since he had already been briefed about the *black roses* being poisonous. Moreover, **Mr. Black Rose** secretly funded and planned the dirty nukes, and the United States was not aware of the illegal connection to **Mr. Black Rose**. Furthermore, the undercover Navy SEAL team eliminated all the rebels in one quick ambush and clandestine mission. Interestingly, the legacy media never reported the event. These heroic SEALs adhered to the words of General Douglas MacArthur: **"There is no substitute for victory."**

Additionally, as a result of previous administrations' negotiations in the last thirty-plus years, six former Canadian provinces and territories became five states: Alberta, Saskatchewan, Manitoba, British Columbia, and Northwest Yukon. The Northwest Territories and Yukon Territory combined to be one state. These Canadian provinces and territories left Canada to avoid being under globalist control and tyranny; however, eastern Canadian provinces, such as Quebec and Ontario, were still under globalist domination. Furthermore, the Canadian central government's corruption in the 2020 decade eventually led to the arrest of the Canadian prime minister. Before former Canada was divided into its respective provinces and territories, the Canadian prime minister, like other treasonous world leaders, was executed by firing squad for his treasonous acts after being convicted by a military tribunal; these treacherous world leaders abused their power and violated their oath. The Canadian people discovered Lord Acton's axiom: **"Power tends to corrupt, and absolute power corrupts absolutely."**

The people of Ontario were strongly considering joining the United States; however, the referendum missed by a couple of percentage points since the globalists still had a tremendous amount of power. Unfortunately, too many people in Ontario fell victim to the globalist propaganda from the media that *Mr. Black Rose* funded; too many people only heard what was stated by state-sponsored media. Former Canada was not the only geopolitical change; the 2088 world map had numerous border modifications as a result of countless political transformations over the past sixty-plus years. Unfortunately, the people of Ontario were not the only ones to be ignorant of George Orwell's warning: **"The people will believe what the media tells them they believe."**

By the historical tricentennial 2076 election, the number of states had expanded to sixty-two with a population of 350 million and an electoral college of 902; the three-hundred-year-old country had grown due to the former Canadian provinces and territories gaining their statehood. By the 2072 elections, the

United States had expanded with these seven other states: Puerto Rico, Israel, Venezuela, Iceland, Northern California, Liberia, and Ireland. Northern California petitioned to separate from the rest of California due to significant political differences. Puerto Rico had been a territory for a long time, and eventually the Puerto Ricans decided to petition for statehood. Moreover, Northern Ireland united with Ireland before the Emerald Island acquired statehood; Ireland, had to overthrow the Irish globalist leaders of their country and exit the EU before they requested statehood. The populace was eventually victorious against the unchecked illegal migrants into Ireland and the Irish globalist government; many Irishmen were concerned that the illegal migrants were devastating the Celtic way of life. Many Irish sympathizers from the United States joined the Irish nationalists to assist their cause.

In regard to Israel, the Israelis wanted protection from the Middle East. Many Israelis agreed with the words of John F. Kennedy: **"Israel was not created in order to disappear—Israel will endure and flourish. It is the child of hope and the home of the brave. It can neither be broken by adversity nor demoralized by success. It carries the shield of democracy and it honors the sword of freedom."**

The six former countries that joined the United States requested statehood via referendum and by obtaining congressional approval, except for Venezuela. Venezuela was conquered by the United States in order to remove Venezuelan tyrannical globalist control; Venezuela was a globalist stronghold and previously controlled by the cabal and *Mr. Black Rose.* The United States pulverized the Venezuelan government and military with minimal civilian casualties; President Baros was one of the fighter pilots, call name *Red Tiger*, during the relatively short war. After the eighty-eight-day Venezuelan War, their appreciative, liberated people insisted on joining the United States. The liberated Venezuelans understood the words of Nelson Mandela: **"There is no easy walk to freedom anywhere, and many of us will have to pass through the valley of the shadow of death again and again before we reach the mountaintop of our desires."**

As a result of the United States' expansion for the past sixty-plus years, the United States had states on all continents except Australia and Antarctica; however, the United States had a scientific lab in Antarctica. The fortunate news for the United States was that Australia and New Zealand combined as one democratically free nation and were strong allies of the United States. Luckily, an additional strong military and economic partner was the newly formed Scandinavian Federal Republic, which comprised the following former nations: Sweden, Norway, Denmark, and Finland.

In early September of 2088, Congressman Drakos, Speaker of the House, started impeachment charges against President Baros; Congressman Drakos was directed to do so by *Mr. Black Rose.* Article II, Section 4 of the US Constitution stated who could be impeached: **"The President, Vice President and all civil officers of the United States, shall be removed from office on impeachment for, and conviction of, treason, bribery, or other high crimes and misdemeanors."** The article of impeachment claimed that President Baros's Megadroid Company was fraudulent and liable for the Memorial Day event due to President Baros's fraud and reckless behavior; the California Supreme Court and appellate court were wrong in their legal decision. The House of Representatives impeachment votes went down party lines; the globalists could not convince any nationalist to vote to impeach. Since the Globalist Party controlled the House, the article of impeachment was sent to the Senate. President Baros had the same sentiment as President Andrew Johnson: **"Let them impeach and be damned."**

The Senate received the article of impeachment. Supreme Court Chief Justice Johnathon Robertson would be presiding over the impeachment trial. He was clearly a globalist sympathizer and may have been blackmailed by the deep state; he had allegedly attended Make-Believe Island on several occasions, a suspected location for child trafficking. The island was secretly funded and controlled by *Mr. Black Rose*, who also controlled the globalists. A globalist president appointed Johnathon Robertson; as Chief Justice, he presided over a nationalist-controlled court, 6–3. The Senate agreed to conduct the trial without delay.

At the commencement of the impeachment trial, the prosecution explained that the California Supreme Court and appellate court were legally wrong. They claimed that the acts of the *fighterbots*, which Megadroid Company had manufactured, clearly acted erroneously. The prosecutors repeatedly claimed that Megadroid Company, owned and controlled by President Baros, was, without a doubt, fraudulent, liable, and criminally guilty. The prosecution repeated the California plaintiff's court transcript. The prosecutors claimed that President Baros's Megadroid Company was guilty of worshiping money, resembling Karl Marx's axiom: **"Money is the alienated essence of man's work and existence; this essence dominates him and he worships it."**

Next, the well-prepared defense had its turn. The defense began by stating that this impeachment trial was unconstitutional since the California trial was a civil case and there was never a claim of any criminal violations by the president. The defense brought in the same witnesses and evidence from the California Civil Court and attempted to bring additional evidence discovered by the military. Supreme Court Chief Justice Johnathon Robertson denied additional evidence from the military, claiming that it was speculative and dubious. The military evidence clearly showed videos of the *fighterbots* being reprogrammed by globalist rebels who were advocating for the overthrow of the United States. The defense argued adamantly to no avail. Afterward, both sides expressed their closing arguments, which were summaries of what they claimed. The chief justice asked the senators to vote to impeach or acquit. The vote went down party lines, which meant President Baros was acquitted and not removed. In this instance, this impeachment trial echoed Psalm 118:6: **"The Lord is on my side; I will not fear: what can man do unto me?"**

3.

THE AMENDMENTS

DURING HIS PROSPEROUS first presidential term, President Baros upheld several historic lessons learned from the 2020 and 2030 decades. He continued and maintained the governmental transformation that occurred after the infamous 2020 and 2024 elections. In several of President Baros's speeches, he reminded everyone of Winston Churchill's quote: **"Those that fail to learn from history are doomed to repeat it."** He reminded everyone regularly that tyrannical governments target their political opposition by using lawfare and corruption. In the 2020s, lawfare was used to economically damage a political presidential opponent, President Trump, by requiring him to post nearly half a billion dollars for an excessive summary judgment in order to appeal. In addition, selective prosecution occurred when one party was not charged for possessing top-secret documents and President Trump was. In 2021, the current president was found to have possessed top-secret documents while he was senator and vice president; however, President Trump was charged with possession of top-secret documents even though he had the authority to declassify documents. In addition, the current president was investigated by a special counsel for actions during his time as vice president and senator, and the special counsel claimed he was guilty as charged of unauthorized possession of top-secret documents; however, he was too senile to be convicted. Furthermore, there was a presidential candidate in 2016 who possessed over thirty thousand classified emails and was not charged with a crime. This was clearly selective prosecution. President Baros, as a result of the impeachment trial and the California Civil Court trial, was convinced that the globalists were willing to use lawfare.

After forty of the fifty states had approved an application by two-thirds of the state legislatures, as authorized in the US Constitution, a constitutional amendment convention was held in 2038. This is one of the two constitutionally authorized methods to amend the Constitution. The ratified amendments were a result of over three-fourths of states ratifying them. This convention was formed because the federal government lacked the backbone and will to implement required governmental reform; no one in Washington, DC, was willing to reduce their power. These states reminded the federal government of James Madison's axiom: **"The powers delegated by the proposed Constitution to the federal government are few and defined. Those which are to remain in the State governments are numerous and indefinite."**

Article V of the US Constitution proscribed the two methods to amend the Constitution: **"The Congress, whenever two thirds of both Houses shall deem it necessary, shall propose Amendments to this Constitution, or, on the Application of the Legislatures of two thirds of the several States, shall call a Convention for proposing Amendments, which, in either Case, shall be valid to all Intents and Purposes, as Part of this Constitution, when ratified by the Legislatures of three fourths of the several States, or by Conventions in three fourths thereof..."** Due to the harsh lessons from the corrupt deep state and early twenty-first century elections, the following eleven amendments to the Constitution were added via the 2038 Constitutional Amendment Convention.

The first added amendment: the United States returned to gold- and silver-backed currency; this was created to prevent run-away spending and printing of money. This limited Congress's authority to create money given in Article I, Section 8, Clause 5 of the Constitution: **"To coin Money, regulate the Value thereof, and of foreign Coin, and fix the Standard of Weights and Measures…"** Furthermore, the national debt may never exceed 30 percent of the GDP without state governors' approval. Moreover, the United States government was forbidden to possess only digital currency; all United States currency was required to be backed by gold and silver, and fiat currency was eliminated. This prevented the federal legislatures and senators from just printing paper currency, which inevitably caused inflation and unavoidably triggered an uncontrollable national debt. This also prevented citizens' right to privacy from being violated by the federal government; digital currency clearly resulted in the government knowing all your economic activities and potentially playing Big Brother, which allowed the government to control the present. The amendment understood George Orwell's axiom: **"Who controls the past controls the future. Who controls the present controls the past."** Furthermore, at least 60 percent of state governors had to agree to raise the debt ceiling to exceed 30 percent of the GDP; the Senate was required to have a simple majority to have the governors' vote to increase the debt from 30 percent. The governors then came to the Senate, listened to the reasoning, and then voted. Obviously, the states desired to prevent the federal government from causing uncontrollable national debt and enslaving the populace. The states were reminding the federal government of the words of Thomas Jefferson: **"The several states composing the United States of America are not united on the principle of unlimited submission to their general government."**

The second added amendment: Another highly popular and supported amendment was passed that established term limits for congressional representatives and senators; the president should not be the only elected position at the federal level with term limits. The states and citizens realized that senators and congressmen had no incentive to limit themselves in any area; term limits would only be realized when the states demanded it. The president already had a two-term limit by the Twenty-Second Amendment: **"No person shall be elected to the office of the President more than twice, and no person who has held the office of President, or acted as President, for more than two years of a term to which some other person was elected President shall be elected to the office of the President more than once."** The legislators could only serve two terms in a row and had to sit out from both houses for a minimum of four years; in addition, no one was eligible for legislative or presidential office if they turned eighty-five prior to being sworn into office. This amendment recognized the common sense of Thomas Jefferson: **"Whenever a man has cast a longing eye on offices, a rottenness begins in his conduct."**

The third added amendment: This extremely accepted alteration limited the Supreme Court to only nine justices, with an age limit of eighty-five years. In addition, this amendment assisted in clarifying the role of the Supreme Court in Article III, Section 1 of the Constitution: **"The judicial power of the United States,** shall be vested in one Supreme Court, and in such inferior courts as the Congress may from time to time ordain and establish. The judges, both of the supreme and inferior courts, shall hold their offices during good behaviour, and shall, at stated times, receive for their services, a compensation, which shall not be diminished during their continuance in office." This added amendment *limited the number of justices to only nine.* It was created to prevent packing and politicizing the Supreme Court; packing the court meant adding additional justices over the traditional nine in order to place a justice with the current administration's political agenda and mindset. This amendment specified an age for the justice to retire with reduced political pressure to remain or vacate. Furthermore, this amendment required that all judges must be chosen by the state executive and confirmed by the state senate; the people could elect no state judge. This alteration was a consequence of state judges being more concerned with winning elections than following the law. The goal of this amendment was to live by the words of Herb Kohl, a Wisconsin politician: **"We give Supreme Court justices this freedom because we expect them to remain above the pull of politics, to avoid the effects of public excitement and allow a broader view, not tied to the whims of the majority at a certain moment in history."**

The fourth added amendment: This amendment required that a legislative bill must state what part or parts of the constitution permit and authorize a bill. This amendment assisted Supreme Court justices in understanding the intent of the law by the legislative branch; in addition, this amendment assisted the Supreme Court in knowing which section or sections of the constitution made a particular bill constitutional according to the legislature. In addition, this requirement prevented Congress from having potential spending and other laws that were unrelated to the intent and purpose of the bill; for example, if the bill was about transportation, there could not be additional spending for the purchase of a military base. One of the goals was to have bills on one topic without hidden agendas and spending. Furthermore, this safeguarded the Supreme Court from being a law-making body or activist court. We must strive to adhere to Abraham Lincoln's words: **"We the people are the rightful masters of both Congress and the courts, not to overthrow the Constitution but to overthrow the men who pervert the Constitution."**

The fifth added amendment: This revision increased the number of senators to three from each state. The Seventeenth Amendment repealed Article I, Section 3: **"The Senate of the United States shall be composed of two Senators from each state, elected by the people thereof, for six years; and each Senator shall have one vote. The electors in each state shall have the qualifications requisite for electors of the most numerous branch of the state legislatures. When vacancies happen in the representation of any state in the Senate, the executive authority of such state shall issue writs of election to fill such vacancies: Provided, that the legislature of any state may empower the executive thereof to make temporary appointments until the people fill the vacancies by election as the legislature may direct."** The reasoning behind the additional senators for each state was to prevent a state from being politically neutral or split. Thus, in a two-party system, a state avoided being neutral and having split party loyalty. Furthermore, the additional senators created a greater balance between the *sovereignty of the people* and the *sovereignty of the states* regarding the electoral college. Moreover, the third senator of each state was elected by the legislative bodies of the respective state, which was the original senatorial selection process; this amendment was intended to remind all of the importance of state legislation. This meant that every two years all congressional seats were up for election; furthermore, one senator from each state was up for election or chosen by their state legislators.

The sixth added amendment: This amendment repealed the practice *by mere congressional law* of limiting the House of Representatives to a fixed number of 435 congressmen regardless of population increase or decrease; however, there still was a minimum of one congressman per state. This amendment declared a representative for every half million citizens in a state; if there were 500,001 persons in a state, that state would have two representatives regardless of the population of the country. This amendment was in the spirit of Alexander Hamilton: **"Here, sir, the people govern; here they act by their immediate representatives."**

The seventh added amendment: This constitutional declaration was designed to prevent the horror and lawlessness of the alleged good intentions of the deep-state security state. This anti-surveillance amendment ensured that the government could not surveil a citizen or citizens without a warrant, and citizens had a right to privacy. This was clearly the result of the revealed scandals of the 2020 election and prior corrupt events. Once irrefutable evidence was presented of the large tech megacorporations doing the will of the deep state and federal government, generally via coercion and blackmail, to censor citizens and information, this amendment was pushed and ratified. In addition, numerous popular tech companies, government officials, and media people were tried for treason and racketeering; however, several individuals had reduced sentences for their cooperation, and they had clear evidence of being blackmailed and coerced by the deep state. Furthermore, this amendment required DC to move to Kansas in order to reset the deep state and centralize the federal government. This was the final death blow for both political parties; ironically, the new globalist and nationalist parties were named for their true intentions and goals. This amendment was inspired by the warning of George Orwell: **"There was of course no way of knowing whether you were being watched at any given moment. How often, or on what system, the Thought Police plugged in on any individual wire was guesswork. It was even conceivable that they watched everybody all the time."**

The eighth added amendment: This controversial change was made to prevent a Manchurian candidate from occupying the White House from a corrupt election; many legal experts were divided on this amendment. It recognized that a Manchurian candidate could occupy the White House due to the court system being judicially deliberate and methodically slow; a Manchurian candidate is not loyal to the country that is elected since his loyalty is to another country or cabal that controls him. This amendment was called the *anti-Manchurian amendment.*

Furthermore, this amendment allowed the president of the Senate (usually the vice president) to summon state governors to Congress to reside as jurors in a corruption trial, after the Supreme Court established a two-thirds majority vote that the election had potentially been corrupted. After being presented with evidence by the president of the Senate, the Supreme Court determined whether the alleged winner should be tried. The president of the Senate was required to present reliable evidence from a dependable source, such as the intelligence agency or military; the Supreme Court then acted as a grand jury and declared whether the alleged presidential winner and their vice presidential candidate should face trial. A two-thirds majority vote of the Supreme Court was required for the president of the Senate to request the governors. The president of the Senate was required to delay the electoral vote count until the corruption trial was completed, which had to be resolved by May 1 of the year following the election.

However, the purpose of the amendment was not to disrupt the presidential selection process. In order to maintain the balance of power, the Senate and House of Representatives could prevent the president of the Senate from exercising this *Anti-Manchurian amendment* if both houses agreed by a three-fifths majority. Even if the Supreme Court had a two-thirds majority, the original election results would stand; however, both houses were required to vote prior to the commencement of the corruption trial. The reason for not requiring merely a simple majority from each house was the fact that the corrupt 2020 election had senators and congressmen who were being blackmailed by the deep state.

The acting president would be determined by the House of Representatives as prescribed by the US Constitution, Article II, Section 1: **"But in chusing the President, the Votes shall be taken by States, the Representation from each State having one Vote; A quorum for this Purpose shall consist of a Member or Members from two thirds of the States, and a Majority of all the States shall be necessary to a Choice."** The acting president could be the current president if he or she was not chosen to be tried in the corruption trial. The Supreme Court would have original jurisdiction, and the chief justice would conduct the corruption trial; however, if the chief justice were conducting another trial, then the most senior justice would conduct the legal proceedings; the chief justice or senior justice would be the judge, and the governor of each state would be the jury. Simultaneously, the military would conduct another provisional election to validate election integrity; however, this election result would be contingent on a guilty verdict of the alleged winner of the original presidential election. If three-fourths of the governors that stood as jurors determined that the election was corrupt, then the guilty individual or individuals could be barred from ever holding an office again. The guilty person could be tried again in a federal or state court for fraud or other felonies. Moreover, if other countries were involved, guilty persons and accomplices could be tried for treason, with a guilty verdict resulting in the death penalty; martial law was not necessarily required for the military, in this instance, to conduct a military tribunal. This was another warning by George Orwell: **"A people that elect corrupt politicians, imposters, thieves and traitors are not victims...but accomplices."** In addition, this amendment required that all citizens show a valid national ID in order to vote for a federal election; the post office and other federal agencies were soon capable of issuing national IDs; globalist-controlled states refused to follow this requirement.

The ninth added amendment: The intent was to limit income tax and corporate tax to a maximum percentage. This amendment was to constrain the Sixteenth Amendment: **"Congress** shall have power to lay and collect taxes on incomes, from whatever source derived, without apportionment among the several states, and without regard to any census or enumer- ation." Both forms of taxation were maximized at 30 percent and required to be a flat tax. This limited-tax amendment was to prevent the federal government from overtaxing as a conse- quence of their reckless spending. This was a result of learning from Milton Friedman: **"Higher taxes never reduce the deficit. Governments spend whatever they take in and then whatever they can get away with."**

The tenth added amendment: This amendment guaranteed that a president had presidential immunity while in office and after office. This legal immunity could only be removed if the president was impeached and found guilty by the Senate. The purpose of presidential immunity was to prevent an opposition state DA or others from charging a former president with civil and criminal indictments for questionable and unpopular acts; without immunity (which senators and congressmen already had), the president would fear acting in several legally unclear cir- cumstances due to fear of political prosecution after leaving office. Admittedly, the Supreme Court had recognized a distinction between personal and official acts; however, a president's actions were assumed official until proven beyond a reasonable doubt to be personal; ironically, they emphasized that a personal act is not necessarily criminal. Furthermore, this amendment guaranteed that a president was treated as a federal officer and was not subject to state-law violations as president.

The eleventh added amendment: This constitutional transfor- mation guaranteed that no judge could issue a gag order on a defendant. Gag orders were legally unwarranted since there were laws established that a defendant could not violate. In other words, it was illegal for a defendant to threaten jury members. Gag orders resulted in violating a defendant's First Amendment rights. This modification resulted from the obvious lawfare of the 2024 presidential election. President Trump was gagged from responding to witnesses and prosecutors' attack on him. Ironically, President Trump, who was gagged, could not react to attacks from witnesses who were not silenced; this affected his campaigning as well. Paradoxically, one of the witnesses was a convicted, disbarred perjurer. In addition, former President Trump was eventually found guilty via a kangaroo-shamed court; the DA resurrected statutorily expired misdemeanors by unproven and unidentified felonies. In other words, expired misdemeanors could be enforced if a felony had been proven, but a felony was not proven or established. However, a judge was allowed to gag witnesses in order to protect the rights of the defendant. The reasoning for this amendment was found in the prudence of Ayn Rand's words: **"The smallest minority on earth is the individual. Those who deny individual rights cannot claim to be defenders of minorities."**

In a controversial 7–2 decision, the Supreme Court determined that property tax was unconstitutional since the "power to tax" meant the power to regulate, control, and eliminate, which was similar to the reasoning for why churches were not taxed; in addition, property tax was a duty on a tax if there were other excises such as sales tax. The court reasoned that the federal, state, or local government could take your property, especially real land, because you did not earn enough money to pay the annual property tax, which meant you were always in debt to the government and truly never owned your land, real property. Furthermore, property tax could increase over time to a significantly larger portion of the original purchase price because of increased property assessments; this was based on the fact that your property tax was based on the assessed value, even if you had no intention ever to sell. In addition, the court ruled that if the property was taken to pay a tax, the government could not profit from seizing the property; in other words, if the property was worth one hundred thousand dollars and the debt was ten thousand dollars, then the ninety thousand dollars must go back to the original owner; the government could not profit from it. The court learned from the wise words of George Washington: **"Freedom and Property Rights are inseparable. You can't have one without the other."**

In another controversial 6–3 ruling, the Supreme Court concluded that the commerce clause must be limited; the commerce clause should not be a superhighway for all federal regulations. It is stated in Article I, Section 8 of the Constitution: **"To regulate commerce with foreign nations, and among the several states, and with the Indian tribes..."** Thus, this judicial act resulted in the reduction of the influence of agencies' regulatory power. This judicial decision emphasized that intrastate commerce must have significance, and there must be limitations to the commerce clause. Moreover, the court determined that a state had the right to regulate its own intrastate commerce; this meant that the state law could supersede the federal regulations for intrastate commerce. In addition, the federal government could not just argue any influence or effect to claim regulatory authority. The court was influenced by these wise words of Alexander Hamilton: **"The State governments possess inherent advantages, which will** ever give them an influence and ascendancy over the National Government, and will forever preclude the possibility of federal encroachments. That their liberties, indeed, can be subverted by the federal head, is repugnant to every rule of political calculation."

As a result of injuries and deaths from mandatory experimental vaccines during the 2020 decade, the Supreme Court ruled 8–1 that the Nuremberg Code's ten points were guaranteed rights for all Americans, and corporations and governmental agencies that had required vaccines for employment were held liable; in addition, these violators could be held criminally accountable. As stated in the Nuremberg Code: **"The voluntary consent of the human subject is absolutely essential."** It was discovered that animal experiments were not done properly or data was manipulated to show vaccines in a more positive light. Furthermore, there was a lack of transparency about the harm of injecting vaccines. It is stated in the Nuremberg Code: **"No experiment should be conducted where there is an a priori reason to believe that death or disabling injury will occur; except, perhaps, in those experiments where the experimental physicians also serve as subjects."** In addition, there was mixed messaging from experts regarding COVID-19 protocols, including differing recommendations on the number of vaccine injections and mask-wearing. Moreover, several courts across the country in the 2030s ruled that the COVID-19 vaccines did not fit the traditional definition of vaccines. There were also reports of arrests of individuals claiming to be COVID-19 experts, as it was proven that the virus originated from a weapons program in Wuhan, China, that was funded by the deep state. Furthermore, the so-called experts and authorities of the 2020 pandemic did not learn from Historian John M. Barry, author of *The Great Influenza: The Story of the Deadliest Pandemic in History*: **"In 1918 the lies of officials and of the press never allowed the terror to condense into the concrete. The public could trust nothing and so they knew nothing. Society is, ultimately, based on trust; as trust broke down, people became alienated not only from those in authority, but from each other."**

The most significant modification to the federal government was that the District of Columbia moved to Kansas in order to be more geographically central to the continental United States; this had the military advantage of protecting the capital from incoming enemy missiles; this relocation included a modernized White House, Capitol, Supreme Court building, and other governmental buildings. Furthermore, it gave greater access to the capital for a greater number of citizens and states throughout the continental United States. Moreover, this DC relocation allowed the deep state to be reset and the agencies to be reorganized. This was from learning from Thomas Sowell: **"Government agencies have their own self-interest to look after, regardless of the interests of those for whom a program has been set up."**

The established seventy-six-square-mile district did not allow any permanent residence. All individuals who served or worked in the district were required to have their primary residency in a state; thus, no one could reside there except during their time in federal office. Furthermore, agency headquarters were spread throughout the country; this prevented the concentration of power from the alleged deep state. In addition, a significant number of agencies were reduced, and these governmental duties were reserved for the states. Several small, ineffective federal agencies were eliminated or absorbed into larger agencies, which significantly reduced the bureaucracy and administrative nature of the federal government. In addition, several well-known agencies, such as the IRS, CIA, and FBI, were substantially overhauled and revised. The constitutional convention learned from Ayn Rand's foresight: **"A proper government is only a policeman, acting as an agent of man's self-defense, and, as such, may resort to force only against those who start the use of force...government that initiates the employment of force against men who had forced no one... reverses its only moral purpose."**

In the United States, the globalist-controlled states modified several of their election laws similar to the corrupt presidential 2020 election; these states changed their election laws by orders from judges to respective globalist governors for the so-called *common good and safety of their people*; the laws were not modified according to the constitution, which required that the state's respective legislative body change election laws. Article I, Section 4, Clause 1 of the United States Constitution stated: **"The Times, Places and Manner of holding Elections for Senators and Representatives, shall be prescribed in each State by the Legislature thereof; but the Congress may at any time by Law make or alter such Regulations, except as to the Places of chusing Senators."** These globalist states, which controlled 35 percent of the electoral college, insisted on lockdowns to mandate online voting or collecting votes via *voterbots*; these lockdowns meant that people were required to remain in their homes, which meant they could only vote via *voterbots* or online. These bots visited everyone. ***Mr. Black Rose*** funded all these efforts and purchased the *voterbots* for the globalist states. Those who opposed online voting and *voterbots* insisted that these methods were inherently vulnerable; these vulnerabilities included hacking and lack of voter verification that eventually led to individuals voting more than once or voting by ineligible voters. In addition, those opposed to *voterbots* remembered what was discovered after the 2020 election: CEOs of voting machine companies were imprisoned for creating machines designed to manipulate and produce predetermined results. The nationalist-controlled states kept their states open for business and did not alter any of their election laws; this included paper ballots with receipts and individually required voter identification cards with a personal PIN number. The corrupt globalists believed that elections were for them and disagreed with Abraham Lincoln: **"Elections belong to the people."**

The globalist-controlled states had voting robots with electronic ballot pads, called *voterbots*, to meet potential voters and encourage people to vote; this occurred as early as thirty days before election day. In addition, there was a limited paper trail for approximately 25 percent of the votes; the vast majority of votes were transmitted electronically from the *voterbots* to the voting precinct; ironically, the globalist states endorsed and advocated for converting *servicebots* to *voterbots*, even though Baros's Megadroid Company manufactured the *servicebots*. A significant number of globalists and **Mr. Black Rose** agreed with Joseph Stalin: **"It doesn't matter who they vote for, they always vote for us."**

Paradoxically, nearly 15 percent of the population from globalist states migrated to nationalist-controlled states. It should have been greater; however, over 45 percent of the nation's workforce worked purely remotely in hybrid work situations;

the remote workforce in general was not as severely affected by the draconian lockdowns as workers who had occupations that required alternate work locations. Moreover, upper-middle-class families and more affluent families had over 80 percent of their children homeschooled by *tutorbots* and online learning; home-school organizations and private schools who cooperated with them provided homeschooled students the opportunity to participate in extracurricular activities from sports to social clubs. On a positive note, families that were able to work from home were creating increased family bonds. The nationalist-controlled states did not close down businesses or require online schooling. Unexpectedly, there were no significant death-rate differences among the states; statistically and scientifically speaking, the draconian laws in the globalist-controlled states were not justifiable. Those who opposed the draconian laws understood English mathematician and biostatistician Karl Pearson's axiom: **"Statistics is the grammar of science."**

President Baros insisted that each state should determine their own legislative response and plans for the new Doggam pandemic, which was suspected to originate from North Korea. He believed that each state was affected differently by the Doggam pandemic. He reminded everyone of the Ninth Amendment: **"The enumeration in the Constitution, of certain rights, shall not be construed to deny or disparage others retained by the people."** The inspiring speech included the Tenth Amendment: **"The powers not delegated to the United States by the Constitution, nor prohibited by it to the states, are reserved to the states respectively, or to the people."** However, he strongly advocated that lockdowns of businesses and schools would guarantee that the cure would be way worse than the disease; he reminded everyone that the adverse effects of the COVID-19 response in the 2020s took over a generation to recover. He retold everyone that the United States was a constitutional federal republic, and he advocated that the federal government should not violate state rights and sovereignty. President Baros strongly advocated adherence to James Madison's words: **"The powers delegated by the proposed Constitution to the federal government are few and defined. Those which are to remain in the State governments are numerous and indefinite."**

Senator Cain, serving his fifth term, argued that the federal government should respond to the pandemic similarly to China, which insisted on completely eliminating the Doggam virus. He strongly believed that the government should have extensive control over the people, and he shared the same beliefs as Carl Flight, who was a supporter of globalist causes and a billionaire. Carl Flight, like Senator Cain, agreed with Karl Marx's favorite quote from Mephistopheles, a character from Goethe's *Faust*: **"Everything that exists deserves to perish."**

Marxist China's reaction had been utterly ruthless and tyrannical, with the Chinese president advocating for and insisting on zero virus. Zero-virus proponents advocated the complete removal of the disease, which is an impossible goal. The unfortunate population had been under a draconian lockdown enforced by a police state. Chinese citizens were executed if they left their domicile without governmental approval. China was now a total-surveillance tyrannical government with mandatory biovalidation of all its citizens. Every Chinese citizen's bio information was known by the state. Furthermore, China controlled its population with merciless, heartless robots. The cruel robots, alias *roboterminators*, had terminated millions of Chinese citizens. Currently, there seemed to be no end to these tyrannical actions. As a result of ruthless governmental actions and disinformation, China's population was under 600 million, less than half of its population in 2020. Ironically, the CCP claimed that the *roboterminators* inadvertently eliminated a hundred thousand CCP members on so-called RED Monday. Suspiciously, these CCP members disagreed with the Chinese president's pandemic agenda. These despicable acts reflected the words of Joseph Stalin: **"Death solves all problems, no man, no problem."**

Senator Cain, who had never worked in the private sector except as a lobbyist (when he was required to sit out for four years between terms), advocated for sending stimulus money to all residents. Of course, this money would come from printing additional currency. This would obviously lead to inflation and potentially deceptive *greedflation*: a situation in which companies took advantage of inflation by significantly increasing their prices beyond inflation levels. Senator Cain loved to retell others Alan Greenspan's words: **"The United States can pay any debt it has because we can always print money to do that. So, there is zero probability of default."** In addition, Senator Cain, like his running mate, Carl Flight, believed that the globalists could create a utopia on Earth in order to fulfill the goal of secular globalutopianism. He and Carl Flight disagreed with Karl Popper, a philosopher, when he said: **"The attempt to make heaven on earth invariably produces hell."**

The Doggam pandemic was estimated to affect 5 to 10 percent of the world population, especially people with morbidities such as obesity and diabetes or elderly people, similar to the historical COVID-19 pandemic; however, the number of deaths from the suspicious disease was in question since some medical experts were claiming that the lion's share of 2087 and 2088 deaths were misdiagnosed. The disease was called Doggam since the disease originated in North Korea. There were claims that Doggam was artificially made in a bio lab, possibly under a weapons program in North Korea, which was similar to the COVID-19 discovery; the bio lab was suspected to be controlled by the CCP and funded by a globalist cabal. President Baros called Doggam the Korean disease since the disease came from North Korea, and Doggam meant 'flu' in Korean.

At several campaign rallies, President Baros expressed, "We are repeating the horrible historical events of the 2020 election. This is why the defunct political parties from the past serve as important historical lessons. The exposed corruption brought the country together, leading to over sixty years of progress and a revival of American principles, all in adherence to the constitution." President Baros reminded all of the wise words of George Santayana, an American philosopher: **"Those who cannot remember the past are condemned to repeat it."**

Senator Cain had a powerful grasp on the globalist-controlled states, like his vice presidential running mate, Carl Flight. The country was clearly divided and highly polarized. Over the years, citizens tended to move to a state that adhered to their political beliefs and values. For example, adults over thirty in a nationalist state were twice as likely to be married or have at least two kids than in a globalist state; nationalist states had less than one-third the number of single parents in globalist states.

Ironically, the states were polarized economically to an under-standable difference; the nationalist-controlled states produced over 75 percent of the GDP and over 80 percent of energy and food. The globalist-controlled states were similar to failed countries such as China, North Korea, former Venezuela, and the former USSR; their unemployment rate was over 15 percent, and over 33 percent received family assistance. Furthermore, Senator Cain's solution was to increase taxes on the nationalist states, which his running mate, Carl Flight, concurred with. President Baros reminded everyone of Margaret Thatcher's epigram: *"The problem with socialism is that you eventually run out of other peoples' money."*

4.

THE QUESTIONABLE
ELECTION

A COUPLE OF WEEKS BEFORE the presidential election, President Baros had an emergency meeting with his military staff. He directed the military through a presidential executive order to monitor the election. If certain conditions occurred, then the military was to spearhead and execute *Operation Integrity*, which was intended to ensure that the election would be fair and lawful. This operation would follow the *Uniform Code of Military Justice (UCMJ)*. Admiral Sarah Davis expressed, "Sir, we shall guarantee that the constitution and our way of life are preserved." President Baros reminded the staff of Samual Adams's wise words: **"The liberties of our country, the freedom of our civil constitution, are worth defending against all hazards: And it is our duty to defend them against all attacks."**

A few days before the 2088 election, President Baros was with his family for a sumptuous dinner, which was the first break from the turmoil in a long time for the entire family. His son, Father Theodore, said grace and thanked God for bringing the family together. Chef Rosa, with the assistance of Butler Charles and *Servicebot Cook*, prepared a traditional Chinese dinner; it was Li Jing's favorite, *jiao zi* (dumplings) and brown rice.

Servicebot Maid brought out the meal and said, "Bon appetit."

Li Jing made her family promise not to discuss the election or politics and only discuss family concerns. Sean stole the show by proudly explaining how he and his Saint Daniel University Roaring Lions football team won their conference championship with a last-second touchdown; the team was undefeated with twelve wins. He, as the quarterback, threw for three touchdowns and passed for 316 yards. After the game, Sean's team awarded him the game ball, which he presented to his mom.

Li Jing delightfully responded, "Sean, thank you. However, you keep the football. I only desire pictures." Sean then gave the football to his girlfriend, Mariana.

Next, Teresa spoke up. Teresa and Sofia were juniors at Saint Peter Catholic High School. Teresa charmingly stated, "I was with Mariana, who was a cheerleader at the game. She was annoyingly bragging about him as usual since their football team will be in the Division 2 football playoff. By the way, our girls' basketball team is undefeated with five wins." Finally, they all congratulated Rex, as the fullback for the Saint Peter football team, for winning their 3A sectional championship game.

Two days before the election, the Maxploration Company was conducting a rocket launch to Mars. This historical launch had eight astronauts who would be the first humans on Mars; interestingly, these extraordinary cosmonauts were four married couples, each conveniently in the same profession: engineers, physicists, doctors, and scientists. As a result of scientific progress, the awesome spaceflight would be approximately seven-plus weeks. Furthermore, the Maxploration Company invented a force field that would shield astronauts from radiation and solar winds. The impressive metallic spacecrafts, called *MAX-200K*, would travel over two hundred thousand miles per hour, which was eight times the speed of spacecrafts in the 2020s. *MAX-200K* would launch to the moon first in order to refuel and resupply, since a tremendous amount of fuel is needed to escape Earth's gravity and the moon's gravity is one-sixth of the Earth's; the moon station, which both astronauts and *spacebots* operate, would be a short stay. Furthermore, previous launches had been made to leave supplies and fuel on the moon. Once at the designated orbit circling Mars, the patriotically painted *MAX-200K* would dock at the Martian Planetary Space Lab that was orbiting Mars for approximately a week. Finally, the astronauts would shuttle to Mars for a one-year tour. The Martian space exploration dream in Buzz Aldrin's adage was being fulfilled: **"Globalization means many other countries are asserting themselves and trying to take over leadership. Please don't ask Americans to let others assume the leadership of human exploration. We can do wonderful science on the Moon and wonderful commercial things. Then we can pack up and move on to Mars."**

As the 2088 election day commenced, regrettably, there were intense riots and ferocious protests in globalist-controlled cities and states; the legacy media stubbornly claimed that it was mostly non-violent and tranquil as the cities and suburbs burned down. These relentless violent acts seemed to be targeting the voting precincts that had a majority of nationalist voters. The pugnacious protestors targeted and wasted the *voterbots* in these rioting precincts, which ultimately resulted in voter suppression; this was a fact since other voting methods were inadequate in the globalist-controlled states. This clearly had a greater effect on the presidential election, where projected margins were only 1 to 4 percent for President Baros. Unfortunately, the climate of the election resembled the quote of Leon Trotsky: **"Under all conditions, well-organized violence seems to him the shortest distance between two points."**

As the polls were reporting their results throughout the country, President Baros jumped to an early commanding lead. As hours passed, President Baros was close to clinching the presidency. Only five states remained undeclared. President Baros needed merely one of those five states to win; furthermore, two additional states were declared for Senator Cain and were beginning to lean toward President Baros. These two states were definitely declared too early, since they flipped back to the president around 9:15 p.m. Moreover, the legacy media was definitely revealing their biases by being outright melancholic and expressing hopelessness. Around 9:30 p.m., all seven states were significantly trending toward the president; at least three of these states statistically had a 99-percent certainty of being placed in President Baros's column. If any one of the seven states went for President Baros, then he would be the president-elect.

The election commentator disappointedly stated on one of the major media networks, "According to our statistical election analyst, President Baros has over a 99-percent chance to win. This analysis is substantiated by a prediction similar to the other statistical analyses of the other major networks. This presidential race is basically over." For some anomalous reason, in all seven states, key globalist-controlled voting precincts declared that their precinct would be closed and the counting of votes would resume at 5:00 a.m. tomorrow. There was no explanation as to why the precincts ceased counting the ballots.

The day after the November 2088 election day, the bewildered country surprisingly awoke to an unexpected suspicious victory of the globalists' presidential candidate over the popular incumbent. The major networks, who ordained themselves as masters of truth, unanimously declared the globalist presidential candidate Cain the winner; President Baros still refused to concede. President Baros was clearly convinced that the dubious election was fake and stolen, like the infamous and fraudulent 2020 election was eventually discovered to be. Immediately, President Baros contacted all seven governors and requested that they find additional legal votes that would flip the state to his favor, as well as to investigate if there was any election fraud; five states agreed to investigate.

President Baros claimed to possess conclusive and definitive evidence of election cheating; however, he did not reveal it to his cabinet or Vice President Andrea Argento. The vice president and some of President Baros's cabinet members were genuinely encouraging President Baros to accept the results. During a cabinet meeting, President Baros responded, "Let me strive to understand your recommendation. On the evening of the election, around 10:00 p.m., for some unexplained reason the counting in seven major metropolitan areas supposedly ceased. Of course, all seven major metropolitan areas are controlled by the Globalist Party, as well as their respective states. My desperate opponent needed to gain at least forty thousand votes in five of these states and ten thousand votes in two of the states in order to win. Coincidentally, when the precincts reopened at 5:00 a.m., my unbelievably lucky opponent was in the auspicious lead after miraculously running the table. Ironically, from 10:00 p.m. to 5:00 a.m., there should have been no counting. I believe that he was playing with a few aces up his sleeve. I would accept the consequences of the election if I believed that there was no cheating." He reminded his staff of Sophocles' witticism: **"Things gained through unjust fraud are never secure."**

As the president's staff was meeting, a colonel from the recently built Hexagon military building interrupted the president and handed him a sealed document; the monolithic Hexagon that replaced the Pentagon was the six-sided military headquarters for all six military services. President Baros examined the document quickly and then placed it back in the yellow envelope marked top secret.

The vice president asked, "Sir, is it anything of immediate concern?" The president said nothing. Without revealing any emotions, he immediately ended the meeting. The vice president thought that the president's silence was extremely unusual and odd.

On every major network, the echoed message was alarmingly the same. The legacy mass media overwhelmingly declared Senator Cain the winner. The media, seemingly unanimously and without question, proclaimed that the election was fair and flawless; they professed that there was no reason to question the election results. Furthermore, they boasted that President Baros should concede and accept the outcome; they repeated that President Baros was purely arrogant and entitled. A well-known legacy commentator emphatically stated, "Marcus Baros, a typical disconnected elitist hectobillionaire and a fanatic religious capitalist, must accept the democratic results; Congress should certify the electors and not recognize any alternate electors. Baros should be removed from office if he tries to rally his supporters."

The Baros family was gathering for dinner and to discuss personal concerns at Baros Manor; additionally, they desired a well-deserved respite from the political turmoil of the country. After Father Theodore said grace, they immediately congratulated Sean for the Roaring Lions football team winning the first game of the Division 2 playoff.

Mariana, Sean's girlfriend of several years, bragged about his football accomplishments. The undefeated team had racked up their thirteenth victory. She highlighted that Sean scored two rushing touchdowns and dashed for 108 yards, but then he threw for 358 yards. Mariana explained as the college's head cheerleader that the fans loved the game and cheered throughout it; it seemed as if the entire Saint Daniel Roaring Lions student body was there. Mariana said that the game reminded her of the euphoria of when Sean's high school team won the state championship his senior year in Indianapolis (Sean and Mariana graduated from Saint Peter Catholic High School). Mariana was one year younger than Sean; however, she was two grades behind him since Sean had skipped a grade.

As the family recognized and listened to Sean and Mariana, the long-serving and well-loved Butler Charles, along with two *servicebots*, brought out his famous roast beef dinner with mashed potatoes and gravy. Butler Charles and Rosa exemplified Italian fashion designer Elsa Schiaparelli's belief: **"Eating is not merely a material pleasure. Eating well gives a spectacular joy to life and contributes immensely to goodwill and happy companionship. It is of great importance to the morale."**

Obviously, Teresa was next to chime in; she bragged about Sofia and her basketball performance. She enthusiastically articulated, "Well, my awesome basketball coach is delighted with me being the point guard like last year. He is ecstatic that we are still undefeated." Teresa and Sofia were faithful admirers of basketball Coach John Wooden, who said: **"Winning takes talent, to repeat takes character."**

They consoled Rex since the Saint Peter football team lost in the 3A regional game. Rex rushed for over one hundred yards and scored two touchdowns in the losing effort. Fortunately for Rex, he had a chess tournament the following day. He was the top chess player for his team, and he had an unbelievable knack for any board game; Li Jing claimed that he was a chess guru. Luckily, the Saint Peter chess team won their fourth chess tournament of the year. Rex lived up to chess grandmaster Bobby Fischer's sentiment: **"Chess and me, it's hard to take them apart. It's like my alter ego."**

After a pleasant gathering and feast, Sean and Mariana departed to watch a newly released action movie with their security guards; of course, Teresa decided to tag along. Obviously, this meant that Mariana's sister, Sofia, would come as well; Sofia and Teresa were best friends. They were both the starting guards for the girls' basketball team. Li Jing gave them all a hug and a kiss. Li Jing treated Mariana and Sofia as daughters; at times, they loved going shopping together with Mariana's mom.

Mariana and Sean had known each other for over eight years. When Sean announced to his family a few years ago that he and Mariana were courting, his family proclaimed that they already knew. Sean was delighted that his family approved of this and loved Mariana. Li Jing joked frequently that if they broke up, they would adopt Mariana. Mariana, Sean, and a few friends had been together through their time at Saint Peter High School and were currently at Saint Daniel University; Li Jing called the devoted long-term friends the Gang of Five since they were seemingly always together.

The Baros Estate was located on a two-square-mile plot in a rural area north of Indianapolis. The lavish Baros estate was named Baros Manor; it included a spacious three-story mansion that resembled a grand white medieval castle; at night, the spacious castle was well-illuminated. The estate, a paragon of wealth, was well-secured with *guardbots* and additional security. The estate was surrounded by a spectacular wall with only two impressive golden gates with the letter B. In the front of the mansion, there is a splendid water fountain. In the rear, there was an Olympic-sized pool with an elegant flower garden and a nine-hole golf course; this was Marcus's private practice course. On the far end of the estate, there was a horse barn next to a cozy bungalow and an idyllic lagoon. In addition, there was an impressive rifle range and a well-laid-out disc-golf course through the forest. Sean and Rex relished shooting at the range; Teresa and Mariana enjoyed a good equestrian event on occasion. Of course, Rex regularly practiced at the disc-golf course with his teammates.

After his darling mom left, Walter expressed with compassion, "Dad, we should fight this. We should bring this to the people. We should divide up the family and have rallies in all seven disputed states. We should contact NGOs and state AGs that are willing to investigate this."

As *Servicebot Cook* brought beverages, Lori responded, "Walter is absolutely correct. Dad, I truly believe that they defrauded the country, and we must discover how they did it."

They continued to discuss it thoughtfully. The family decided to have rallies in all seven disputed states and the territories of Greenland and Greece; however, they concurred that they should do it as two- or three-family-member teams at each rally; in addition, President Baros desired to be at most of them. Of course, they all understood that Teresa, Rex, and Sean should not attend the rallies since they should focus on school. Li Jing's tiger-mom educational demands guaranteed that her children would exceed her and heed Leonardo da Vinci's warning: **"Poor is the pupil who does not surpass his master."**

President Baros participated in a well-attended Veterans Day affair at the Hexagon. The occasion was extremely patriotic and moving, with the recognition of the unknown soldier and military service. President Baros presented an excellent speech that emphasized the famous words of General Douglas MacArthur: **"Duty, honor, country: Those three hallowed words reverently dictate what you ought to be, what you can be, what you will be."** The legacy media mocked the president for attending this veteran event; the globalists and elites ridiculed any actions that evoked patriotism, traditional religion, or family values. The media was averse to Ronald Reagan's words: **"[Our goal] is to help revive America's traditional values: faith, family, neighborhood, work and freedom. Government has no business enforcing these values, but neither must it seek, as it did in the recent past, to suppress or replace them. That only robbed us of our tiller and set us adrift. Helping to restore these values will bring new strength, direction, and dignity to our lives and to the life of our nation. It's on these values that we'll best build our future."**

The first spectacular al fresco rally in Calgary, Alberta, had a presidential-vote difference of less than a few thousand votes. There were well over fifty thousand devoted presidential supporters. The biased legacy media, who thought of themselves as the cognoscenti, refused to cover the rally; however, that did not seem to matter since numerous social media outlets covered the event. Lori explained extensively about the accomplishments of her father's first term, as well as questioning the election. She emphasized and questioned why the seven states stopped counting while the other fifty-five states were able to complete and report their counting on election day; in addition, officials of those precincts stated there was no counting between 10:00 p.m. and 5:00 a.m., so how could these states immediately flip when counting started again in all seven states? If the election was conducted honestly and a miracle did occur, then the counting should have taken a couple of hours before any outcome was declared.

President Baros entertained the audience with one-liners and reminded everyone of the terrific accomplishments of the last four years. He stated, "I shall heed a warning to all that are involved in the election corruption; we have the evidence of the fraudulent election. If you turn yourself in and cooperate before the end of the year, you will not be charged with treason and other high crimes." He explained his warning in great depth as the audience repeatedly yelled, **"Lock them up."**

Congressman Drakos, the Speaker of the House, introduced a congressional cease-and-desist order to President Baros in regard to conducting political rallies and enticing civil disturbance, and another congressional cease-and-desist order from stating future fallacious accusations or misinformation about the election results. The House of Representatives' vote for both orders went as expected, which was by party loyalty. President Baros responded by reminding Congress of the separation of powers and that, even as the president, he was entitled to freedom of speech. He reminded everyone of Article II of the Constitution: **"The executive power shall be vested in a President of the United States of America."** He eloquently reminded Congress of James Madison's profound words: **"The accumulation of all powers, legislative, executive, and judiciary, in the same hands, whether of one, a few, or many, and whether hereditary, self-appointed, or elective, may justly be pronounced the very definition of tyranny."**

Two other enormous rallies in Northern California and British Columbia went just as well as Alberta, and the enthusiasm was unbelievable. The presidential-vote differences were similar to Alberta's results, and crowds at the rallies were even grander, especially in Northern California. President Baros emphasized his administrative accomplishment and issued a warning again. Father Theodore reminded everyone at both conventions of the famous words of Albert Einstein: **"The world will not be destroyed by those who do evil, but by those who watch them without doing anything."**

The current leader of the Globalist Party, Congressman Drakos, was drafting articles of impeachment against President Baros once again. His motivation seemed to stem from the animosity and political vendetta that arose after he lost to President Baros in the 2084 election and the previous impeachment attempt failed. Additionally, he was acting under the direction of *Mr. Black Rose*. Congressman Drakos believed that he was robbed of his ultimate destiny, which was promised by his deep-state supporters and benefactors like *Mr. Black Rose*; he was promised to be the next crowned president. Congressman Drakos frequently campaigned and stated that if Baros won, the nation would experience an Orwellian nightmare on its centennial anniversary; globalists like Drakos tended to project by accusation. Ironically, Congressman Drakos wanted to implement George Orwell's nightmare: **"The most effective way to destroy people is to deny and obliterate their own understanding of their history."**

The globalist-controlled House of Representatives was vexed by the protests throughout the country and the increasing popularity of the president. Congressman Drakos and others blamed President Baros for causing public insurrection and civil disturbance. In an undisclosed tête-à-tête sub rosa, Congressman Drakos met with *Mr. Black Rose,* who gave him distinct orders, which included the ultimate goal of secular globalutopianism. *Mr. Black Rose* was a key secret benefactor for the globalists, and very few knew his true identity.

Next, the congressman met with Senator Cain secretly, who did not know what *Mr. Black Rose's* true identity was. Congressman Drakos stated, "I believe that we have this. You must not do anything and avoid making any comments or interviews; you must stay aloof and distant; our backers want you to stay low and avoid the media. You definitely will be sworn in as the next president; besides, our benefactors have our backs and have guaranteed this eventual reality. *Mr. Black Rose* has guaranteed us that the nationalists will fail." *Mr. Black Rose* was a key figure in a secretive global organization. Congressman Drakos reminded Senator Cain of Niccolo Machiavelli's axiom: **"Politics have no relation to morals."**

Two weeks before Thanksgiving, the Saint Peter disc-golf team was one of four teams that qualified for the state championship meet. Of course, the returning state champion team, Saint Michael, also qualified. After nine baskets, the first and fourth were only separated by five throws. Chad, Rex's best friend, threw a hole-in-one on the sixteenth basket. Chad, like Rex, was on Saint Peter's football, lacrosse, and baseball teams as well. Going into the eighteenth basket, Saint Peter and Saint Michael were tied; the other two teams were a distant third and fourth. Ironically, Saint Michael's best player had a bad throw that ended up in the river. This resulted in the Saint Peter Golden Knights winning their first-ever disc-golf state championship. Rex thought that the other team lost because they did not learn from Patrick McCormick's words, author of *Zen and the Art of Disc Golf*: **"Many shots are missed in life because we fail to drop our baggage and give full concentration to our true goals."**

Fortunately, the same weekend, Rex's chess team won the local Catholic chess tournament, with twelve schools participating; Rex was the number one board on the team. When Rex played chess, he adhered to the lessons of Samurai Miyamoto Musashi, a Japanese warrior: **"In battle, if you make your opponent flinch, you have already won."**

At another lovely family dinner, Father Theodore said grace and a special prayer to save the nation from corruption. As *Servicebot Maid* served dinner, Mariana initiated the conversation by bragging about her boyfriend Sean, since their college football team won their quarterfinal game; thus, the Roaring Lions would be playing in the Division 2 semi-championship game after Thanksgiving weekend. She delightfully elaborated on how well Sean performed athletically. He scored the only touchdown in the low-scoring, competitive game. The excellent field-goal kicker booted a last-second winning field goal after Sean marched his team methodically down the field; after the victory, the Roaring Lions' fans stormed the field.

Teresa stated, "The game was awesome! The great news is that, so far, the football games do not interfere with our basketball schedule."

Li Jing congratulated Rex for his chess team winning their sixth tournament in a row; Rex's USFC rating was now 2225, which meant he was a national master. Before everyone departed, Marcus gave them an early family Christmas gift from his Megadroid Company; he presented two sentient robotic dogs named Max and Mega. These advanced, well-trained robotic pets resembled black German Shepherds. Sean, Rex, and Teresa were absolutely delighted with both impressive canines; however, Butler Charles had to remind the *servicebots* that the robotic dogs were part of the family. The family agreed with the sentiment of German Chancellor Otto von Bismark: **"Dogs are not our whole life, but they make our lives whole."**

After the delightful dinner, Mariana and Sean went to a dance at Saint Daniel Catholic University; unfortunately, their security guards and *guardbots* had to go with them. *Servicebot Chauffeur* drove them to the dance. Sofia came over to complete her math and English homework, as well as to practice basketball with Teresa. Sofia and Teresa enjoyed practicing basketball in the Baros's holograph room; this advanced room simulated two three-player basketball teams, which definitely improved their game; moreover, Teresa recruited a couple of *servicebots* in order to play two on two. Of course, the holograph room could simulate other themes, such as a heavenly Chinese garden, which Li Jing relished; she would pore over Chinese poetry or the Bible. Li Jing reminded her family regularly of Confucius's saying: **"Everything has beauty, but not everyone sees it."**

At the standing-room-only campaign assembly in Winnipeg, Manitoba, there was a delay of a few hours due to someone sabotaging the electric transformers supplying power to the event.

Fortunately, this did not cause the president's loyal supporters to leave. The problem was resolved by emergency generators brought to the colosseum. Other than the delay, this spectacular rally was just as successful as the previous ones. There was clearly a national fever and momentum for the president. Even the legacy media had to acknowledge that if the election were held today, President Baros would easily win. However, they still emphasized that he was causing civil unrest and potentially may cause an insurrection. The media would not agree that the current situation was warranted by Mahatma Gandhi's axiom: **"Civil disobedience becomes a sacred duty when the state has become lawless or corrupt. And a citizen who barters with such a state shares in its corruption and lawlessness."**

Congressman Drakos called for an emergency congressional session in order to vote on the three articles of impeachment against the president. The impeachment vote went basically down party line with, surprisingly, six National-Party members joining the globalists. The six nationalist congressmen were expected to have been blackmailed by deep-state operatives; allegedly, the deep state had evidence of nefarious acts or crimes performed by the six congressmen. These despicable acts included honeypots, child trafficking, sexual deviance, and bribes. These alleged blackmails protected the agenda of the deep state; these blackmails were similar to what was discovered after the 2020 election. These six traitorous congressmen and others, similar to Supreme Court Chief Justice Johnathon Robertson, were suspected of traveling to an island that trafficked children for sexual exploitation; this demonic island was nicknamed Make-Believe Island; these criminal acts and blackmail were similar to what was discovered during

the 2020 decade. Congressman Drakos immediately delivered the
impeachment articles to the Senate so that the second impeachment trial could commence as soon as possible.

During the highly controversial and publicized impeachment vote, President Baros was at his White House office;
the modern White House had all the contemporary conve-
niences and all the historical items from the old White House.
Furthermore, the walls of the White House were covered with
the latest technology, smart wallpaper: the nanotechnology
allowed one of the walls in the president's office to transform into
a large screen or be programmed to change to different wallpaper
designs. When President Baros was alone, his predilection was
to have the room resemble a log cabin with a temperate, soothing fireplace. Marcus's personal *servicebot* introduced a colonel
who handed him another top-secret envelope. He perused the
enclosed document and called for an emergency meeting with
his trusted generals and admirals at Baros Manor. The top-secret
documents revealed evidence that the election was stolen and a
globalist cabal was potentially behind it, suspected to be under
the control of a **Mr. Black Rose**.

While the *servicebots* took care of the military staff, the
generals and admirals reviewed a highly confidential document.
They presented convincing video evidence and sworn testimonials revealing that the election had been manipulated and stolen
by globalist forces and funded by **Mr. Black Rose**. Prior to the
meeting, President Baros agreed with his trusted advisor, Admiral
Sarah Davis. She cautioned him against including certain generals and admirals whom she suspected of being untrustworthy
globalists and potentially controlled by **Mr. Black Rose** and the

cabal. Additionally, she suggested inviting Sergeant Major Nika to provide an enlisted perspective. Admiral Sarah Davis reminded the president of Marcus Tullius Cicero's warning: **"A nation can survive its fools, and even the ambitious. But it cannot survive treason from within. An enemy at the gates is less formidable, for he is known and carries his banner openly. But the traitor moves amongst those within the gate freely, his sly whispers rustling through all the alleys, heard in the very halls of government itself."**

A few days after the 2088 Thanksgiving Day at Baros Manor, the Baros family was gathered for a belated Thanksgiving dinner. Father Theodore said grace and thanked God for bringing the family together. Chef Rosa, with the assistance of *Servicebot Cook*, prepared an extravagant, delicious traditional turkey feast with dressing and delicious appetizers. As the *servicebots* were serving, Li Jing insisted that her family promised not to discuss the election or politics and only discussed family issues and accomplishments.

Mariana grabbed the show by proudly describing how Sean and their Saint Daniel Catholic University blue-and-gold Roaring Lions football team won the Division 2 semi-championship by scoring a final rushing touchdown that sealed the win. Sean tossed for two touchdowns and passed for 323 yards. Sean was declared the player of the game.

Lori enthusiastically stated, "Walter and I enjoyed the victory; the Roaring Lions have fifteen wins and zero losses. I am so glad that Mom was able to attend as well."

President Baros said, "Yes, I enjoyed watching the exciting game on the local broadcast network. I especially relished when Sean rushed fifty-two yards for the winning touchdown."

Teresa expressed that she and Sofia loved being at the game; they especially enjoyed observing Sean being honored on the mammoth screen. In addition, Mariana bragged about Sean being on the dean's list again for his engineering grades.

The family also congratulated Sean on his accomplishments last month since many of his family members could not attend. During his Boy Scouts Venturing Court of Honor in early October in Indianapolis, Sean was awarded his Summit Rank before his twenty-first birthday; he was the first in the family to achieve this. Sean loved going on adventures from the National Jamboree to Sea Base. Sean and Mariana were both Venturers and belonged to the same Venture Crew. They went on several adventures together; Mariana earned her Gold Award in Girl Scouts and had been in scouting as long as Sean. On this honorable day, he was recognized for his Ranger Award. The Baros men sentimentally agreed with Robert Baden-Powell, founder of scouting: **"Try to leave this world a little better than you found it and, when your turn comes to die, you can die happy in feeling that at any rate you have not wasted your time but have done your best."**

The family also congratulated Rex. A few weeks ago, the Saint Peter football team had easily won the regional 3A championship 42–0, with Rex scoring three touchdowns and rushing for 198 yards. However, they lost in the semi-state the week before Thanksgiving. The next day after the football team's loss, the Golden Knights disc-golf team remained undefeated, winning three meets that season. In the Indianapolis Catholic disc-golf meet, there were eight private high schools, each with five players on their teams. Rex was the only left-handed disc thrower on the team; however, he was able to throw with his right hand when required. The annual meet took place at a challenging Indianapolis course with eighteen baskets, with sixteen baskets between 200 and 330 feet. There were also two baskets just under 450 feet, including the last basket and the ninth basket. On the eighteenth basket, Saint Peter was trailing by two to their Catholic High School nemesis, Saint Michael, the previous year's state champion. At the previous basket, Rex, on his second throw, landed the winning throw, a double eagle, securing the victory for his team. Rex understood football coach Vince Lombardi: **"Winning isn't everything, it's the only thing."**

As *Servicebot Maid* turned on the stereo to play soothing music, Lori revealed, "My husband Bill and I have some great news. I am a few months pregnant."

Li Jing started crying tears of joy and immediately hugged and kissed her daughter. This would be their third grandchild. Walter and his wife Julia had fraternal twins three years ago. The cherished three-year-olds were a delightful boy and girl who were walking and talking. The gorgeous twins were the center of attention during all their family celebrations. President Baros stated, "God has given us another priceless and beautiful cherished gift. We shall celebrate all our precious gifts this coming Christmas."

Father Theodore said a prayer and blessing. He reminded them of Psalm 127:3: **"Behold, children are a gift of the Lord, The fruit of the womb is a reward."** After congratulating Lori and her husband with warm hugs, Sean and Mariana left for a Sunday night professional football game. Their dedicated security guards were delighted to attend.

Over a week before Christmas, the Baros family, without the president, were at the Division 2 national college football championship game in Indianapolis. Mariana was cheerleading the Roaring Lions fans. Juan, Mariana's brother, scored an impressive running touchdown, which gave Saint Daniel's team the early lead. After a fortuitous fumble, Sean threw a pass to Juan, which gave their team a two-touchdown lead going into the fourth quarter. Their opponent scored with two minutes remaining; however, the Roaring Lions were able to kill the clock and win the Division 2 national college football championship. Father Theodore was proud of Sean's accomplishments since he had prepared religiously. Father Theodore knew that Sean understood Confucius's words: **"Success depends upon previous preparation, and without such preparation there is sure to be failure."**

5.

FULL-FLEDGED LAWFARE

THE SENATE RECEIVED THE ARTICLES of impeachment, all three of which stated that President Baros was impeached for high crimes and misdemeanors by the House of Representatives. The first article claimed that the president *abused his power* by holding rallies to undermine the elections and arouse civil unrest. The second article claimed that President Baros was *guilty of obstruction of Congress* for not ceasing to conduct rallies and false statements about the election when directed not to do so. The third article of impeachment was for President Baros's *interference in the 2088 election* by his insistence on finding additional votes. The Senate responded after informing the Supreme Court that the chief justice would be the judge; the impeachment trial would commence after the Christmas and New Year congressional recess. Chief Justice Johnathon Robertson, who oversaw the first impeachment trial, was ready to do it again. Chief Justice Johnathon Robertson could not have cared less about the reality of Judge Irving Kaufman's saying: **"The Supreme Court's only armor is the cloak of public trust; its sole ammunition, the collective hopes of our society."**

Congressman Drakos regularly told the media that President Baros was another Richard Nixon and a corrupt president. He said President Baros would make the same excuse as Richard Nixon: **" I know you heard what you thought I said, but what I said isn't what I meant."**

President Baros was conducting a legal conference with several well-known constitutional attorneys to prepare for the impeachment trial; the president insisted that the legal team would be funded from his pocket; the president, who donated his presidential salary, did not want to burden the taxpayers with his woes. President Baros insisted that Lori and Walter attend the meeting as well. The constitutional lawyers advised the president that this was primarily a political show trial; these attorneys believed that the constitutional law was on the president's side. They suggested that he be careful what he stated; however, one of the lawyers joked that was not going to happen. Their biggest concern was that Supreme Court Chief Justice Johnathon Robertson was a globalist partisan. In addition, he was allegedly blackmailed by the deep state for frequently attending Make-Believe Island. The deep state refers to unelected bureaucrats, especially those in intelligence agencies, who have the power to control elected officials through blackmail or bribes. Furthermore, several powerful deep-state bureaucrats were under the control of *Mr. Black Rose*.

President Baros stated, "Well, I believe that we have an awesome legal team. I shall warn you that I shall continue to behave and speak as if there was no impeachment trial. Prepare to earn your paycheck."

After the *MAX-200K* spacecraft securely docked and fastened to the enormous Martian Planetary Space Lab, the eight astronauts aboard the space lab were welcomed by four *spacebots* that conducted an informative tour; these heroic astronauts would be the first humans on Mars. The world witnessed the entire spectacular historical event, since a couple of Martian satellites were able to record the events. The *spacebots* were advanced androids manufactured by the Megadroid Company. These talented *spacebots* maintained this remarkable space lab as well as the Martian shuttle. This futuristic and advanced space lab was extremely spacious, with a comfortable capacity for twenty persons; it even possessed two large, well-equipped rooms. One room was for dining, and the other was for exercising or relaxing. Moreover, this space lab was capable of expanding and enlarging by attaching space pods; the *MAX-200K* spacecraft was attached as if it were a space pod, which allowed the *spacebots* to maintain and repair it. The astronauts expressed that they should be on the surface of Mars by New Year's Day.

Commander Planda expressed, "Mr. President, by next year, the United States will be a two-planet nation. We shall plant the United States flag on Olympus Mons, the largest mountain in the solar system."

The commander gave the space command and the president an excellent status report of their current condition. The welcoming *spacebots* had prepared a delicious steak-and-potatoes dinner that was farmed on Mars, which included vintage red wine from Martian gardens. For amusement, the astronauts, with Commander Planda leading, performed Karaoke songs that were televised back on Earth while the technologically advanced room conducted a laser light show. Commander Planda had some of the *spacebots* singing and dancing as well.

The next day, Astronaut Brian Baru played five chess games simultaneously, and he won all five; however, his lovely wife and a *spacebot* gave him a run for his money. Astronaut Brian Baru fulfilled Bobby Fischer's attitude: **"Chess is life."**

The subsequent three rallies in Iceland, Greenland, and Greece occurred simultaneously just before Christmas, and President Baros's family split the effort. All three of these campaigns had similar expected messages and warnings.

In Reykjavik, Iceland, President Baros expressed, "Well, I have been given the great presidential honor of being politically impeached twice and awarded another show trial. Obviously, I am speaking truth to the globalists' power. I am now placed in history with other great presidents who have been impeached unjustly, especially twice; I am willing to stand in their way to protect our way of life."

Of course, the president gave an ultimatum to all involved in corruption, saying that this was their final warning. There would be no deals after the New Year. The audience yelled and chanted, **"Jail them all."**

Walter spoke to a packed, ecstatic crowd at the Nuuk, Greenland, gathering. It seemed as if the entire territory was there. "We, together, shall make Greenland a great state. We shall release your God-given gifts and potential, which will make the great territory of Greenland a bright beacon of hope, freedom, and prosperity. We look forward to Greenland being the sixty-third or sixty-fourth great state."

In Athens, Greece, Lori enthusiastically proclaimed, "After becoming a state, Greece will be the home of the Summer Games."

Even the legacy media conceded that the controversial and allegedly unconstitutional protests were affecting the populace in favor of the president. They even admitted that President Baros's approval rating was over 60 percent; the legacy commentators argued that this was a consequence of the president misleading and lying to the American people.

Ironically, all the legacy media turned on a dime, declaring that the Doggam pandemic was over and everyone could resume their normal lives. The non-legacy media was shocked, as there was no explanation other than government experts and world health organizations stating that it was over. Furthermore, the media advocated that Baros deserved to be impeached again.

The legacy reporters interviewed Congressman Drakos several times. Congressman Drakos emphasized to the reporters that the president was corrupt and should be removed from office; he claimed that Baros was the enemy of democracy and the government. Congressman Drakos stated again that Baros was identical to Nixon, and Baros's actions were explained by Nixon's words: **"I was not lying. I said things that later on seemed to be untrue."**

After attending an elegant and spiritually moving Christmas Mass that Father Theodore conducted, the Baros family was celebrating Christmas at the opulent Baros Manor. The family discussed Father Theodore's sermon, which reminded the parishioners that the Messiah was born; additionally, he thoroughly enlightened them with the significance of Galatians 4:4-5: **"But when the fulness of the time was come, God sent forth his Son, made of a woman, made under the law, To redeem them that were under the law, that we might receive the adoption of sons."**

The family gathered around the Christmas Tree and sang "Silent Night." The family also insisted, like every year, that Butler Charles and Rosa dine with the family, which included the *servicebots*. Every Christmas, Lori and Li Jing assisted their longtime family cook, Rosa, in preparing the Christmas Feast; however, Rosa insisted that Lori take it easy since she was several months pregnant; the great news was that the *servicebots* did most of the extensive labor. The family was delighted that Lori had had an ultrasound, and she informed them that the baby would be a boy.

As *Servicebot Maid* poured drinks, Father Theodore said grace and thanked God for another wonderful family gathering. He emphasized the words from Luke 1:30-32: **"But the angel said to her, 'Do not be afraid, Mary; you have found favor with God. You will conceive and give birth to a son, and you are to call him Jesus. He will be great and will be called the Son of the Most High. The Lord God will give him the throne of his father David...'"**

As the *Servicebots Maid* and *Cook* worked diligently, the family dined on their traditional Christmas feast, which included savory roast beef with mashed potatoes and other Christmas delicacies. During the spectacular dinner, Teresa expressed that she and Rex were on the honor roll again. She thanked Sofia, who was also on the honor roll, with the highest GPA in her junior class, for assisting her in calculus, since Sofia was the best math student in her grade; of course, she thanked *Servicebot Educator* as well. Educator was well-versed in all high school courses and several college freshman courses. They both bragged that they received an A in Father Theodore's calculus class. She also stated that the girls' basketball team was still undefeated. The family congratulated Sean for being the star player of the national championship game, as well as Juan for his exceptional performance. Sean stated that he and Juan would graduate next semester as mechanical engineers; however, both of them planned to attend graduate school at Saint Daniel Catholic University, and both of them had just been accepted. Mariana had two more years of nursing before she graduated; thus, when Sean earned his master's in engineering, Mariana should be finished with nursing college. In addition, like every summer, Juan and Sean would work at Megadroid Company.

After their marvelous feast, the family gathered at the twenty-foot-tall Christmas tree, which was decorated with silver tinsel and ruby-red ornaments; the exquisite Tannenbaum was located near the main entrance. Butler Charles and Rosa always insisted on staying, even after they and others received their annual Christmas bonuses. Besides, Charles and Rosa were married to each other and resided wherever the master and mistress dwelled. Also, Charles and Rosa were happy since their daughter was with them and the Baroses while home from college. The family tradition of gift-giving proceeded from the youngest to the oldest, which meant that President Baros had plenty of time to enjoy imbibing his spiked eggnog.

Ji Ling, as she held her husband, said to him, "We have a wonderful family, and we have lived by Confucius's words:

'The strength of a nation derives from the integrity of the home.'"

Servicebot Chauffeur escorted a colonel to meet the president. Unfortunately, the colonel interrupted the festive event and handed the president another top-secret envelope. The colonel stated, "Mr. President, Merry Christmas to you and your family. I apologize for interrupting your family's Christmas celebration."

The president responded with a Christmas greeting and insisted that the colonel take a bottle of vintage red wine for his family. He told the colonel that he would have a conference call with the same admirals and generals tomorrow night. *Servicebot Maid* bestowed a bottle of wine and a few other gifts on the colonel. President Baros examined the document and smiled with delight. He thought to himself, *Well, this is clearly excellent intel.*

President Baros returned to the family celebration as Sean announced that he had proposed to Mariana in the living room, and she accepted; he had romantically proposed to her on his knees next to the grand fireplace. They planned, with their family's blessings, to marry that summer before he attended engineering graduate school; Mariana would continue her nursing program. Sean asked his brother to perform the wedding, and Father Theodore agreed with a brotherly hug. Li Jing cried tears of joy, since that was what Marcus and Li Jing did after they graduated from college. Lori immediately embraced Mariana and welcomed her to the family. *Servicebot Cook* poured beverages for everyone in order to toast. *Servicebot Maid* turned on the stereo system to play Christmas music.

Marcus immediately responded that he did not want them to struggle while at graduate school; he whispered to his loving wife and told her to assist Mariana in picking out a car and an apartment near the university campus.

Li Jing lovingly smiled and kissed him. She whispered in his ear, "Of course, Dear. I shall also assist Mariana, our future loving daughter-in-law, in choosing an appropriate family car and home near the university. They will not want an apartment; the house must be grand enough for the Gang of Five." He just smirked and shook his head. The family then started playing board games together and singing Christmas Carols.

During a video conference, the generals and admirals briefed the president on additional evidence that clearly brought legitimate questions about the suspicious result of the 2088 election. They mentioned that five whistleblowers or informants, who all admitted to committing election fraud, came forward with significant evidence of corruption; however, two informants unfortunately had been assassinated. They had the other three informants under witness protection with high security. The legacy media had refused to report the deaths of the well-known individuals. President Baros had a private conversation with highly trusted Admiral Davis and Major General Gunner; they had all served together during the Venezuelan War. They concurred on what the next steps should be. Admiral Sarah Davis expressed that they should adhere to the constitution, laws, and UCMJ. President Baros reminded them of Matthew 5:6: **"Blessed are they which do hunger and thirst after righteousness: for they shall be filled."**

President Baros held their annual New Year's Eve celebration in the District of Columbia, Kansas. Teresa, Rex, Mariana, and Sean were able to attend since they were on winter break. *Servicebot Educator* tagged along since he was a great source of information and had a sense of humor. The spectacular event was televised since there would be patriotic music and an extensive fireworks show starting at 11:30 p.m. The president gave an exceptional speech that focused on the future prosperity of the country, which included the recent territories of Greenland and Greece. He reminded all of the inspiring words of Benjamin Franklin: **"Be at war with your vices, at peace with your neighbors, and let every new year find you a better man."** His patriotic, moving speech ended with cannons firing and supersonic fighter jets passing over. Teresa and Rex loved the spectacular climactic fireworks show, which ended with a remarkable light show, with drones spelling out *Happy New Year!*

On New Year's Day of 2089, the eight valorous astronauts landed on Mars; the *spacebots* were televising the entire event. The astronauts planted a United States flag on Olympus Mons.

On a live feed to the president and the world, Commander Planda expressed, "Mr. President, we have safely landed on Mars. We were greeted by the 316 *spacebots* that have been terraforming

Mars and preparing our prodigious Martian Space Station for the astronauts. Of course, they have done a fantastic job preparing for our arrival. We are extremely impressed with how they have taken care of the animals and our delightful pets. By the way, we have some amazing news. Astronaut Sally and her husband will have their first baby in eight months. In addition, my wife is pregnant as well. We will discover who will have the first Martian baby."

After over a four-minute delay due to the immense distance between the two planets, the president responded by congratulating the astronauts and expressing to the world that this historical day would motivate future space exploration.

For the last decade, the remarkable *spacebots* had been working diligently to transform Mars into a second Earth. The terrific news was that Mars' approximately twenty-five-degree tilt and days lasting slightly less than twenty-five hours are similar to Earth, which would assist the astronauts' adaptation to the planet; however, the greatest effort was transforming the atmosphere and increasing Mars' temperature to be more Earth-like. The *spacebots* even resolved other issues, such as acquiring water and shielding from solar winds and rays. The *spacebots* discovered a large water source that was over six-miles deep within Mars, which could have enough water to place the entire Red Planet under a mile of water.

The enormous Martian Station was impressive and magnificent—over one square mile. It was located near the Martian equator, and this square-mile area had a gravitational effect similar to Earth thanks to an advanced gravitational machine that used an enormous amount of nuclear energy. There were numerous pods and technologically advanced buildings connected by tunnels or above-ground tubes. Moreover, there was the first-ever advanced holodeck for astronauts to spend quality time experiencing Earth again and temporarily escaping Martian life. Furthermore, the underground Martian system was impressive since it blocked the solar rays and winds; however, a few years ago, Megadroid developed an artificial magnetic field around Mars. This field was produced by six satellites that orbited Mars and blocked a significant number of solar rays and winds; in addition, the two Martian moons, Phobos and Demos, were equipped to assist in creating this protective field. The astronauts felt they had achieved Buzz Aldrin's when he said: **"Mars is there, waiting to be reached."**

The next day, six astronauts decided to play in the first-ever Mars disc-golf championship, refereed by a couple of *spacebots*. The Mars *spacebots* had already created a nine-basket disc-golf course on Mars' surface with Earth-like gravity; however, the thin atmosphere created a unique experience. The lower air pressure caused the golf disc to stabilize earlier in flight. *Spacebot 17* diligently videoed the entire tournament, which was sent to several networks. The close game was on a delayed broadcast on several sports networks in the United States. Commander Planda clinched the win with an astounding hole-in-one, an eagle at the eighth basket, and an impressive birdie throw at the ninth basket. Astronaut Planda and one other astronaut, chess grandmaster Brian Baru and former commander of the Alpha-Omega Space Lab, were Indiana disc golfers ranked in the top ten. Commander Planda adhered to the advice of Bobby Knight: **"Your biggest opponent isn't the other guy. It's human nature."**

In the city of Regina, Saskatchewan, the gathering was packed, with standing room only; the assembly hall was enormous and grand. At the last moment, President Baros was not able to attend since he had an emergency meeting with his military staff. There was a temporary blackout, which was quickly resolved with pre-planned backup generators. When the rally commenced, Walter Baros spoke with clarity and focus. He expounded how the government must reduce unnecessary and invasive regulations and taxes in order to unleash our American ingenuity and inventiveness. He emphasized Ronald Reagan's words: **"Government is not a solution to our problem, government is the problem."** He recapped his father's accomplishments for the enthusiastic crowd, and these accomplishments were just the beginning. He reminded the crowds that a free-market system would unlock the country's economic potential. He quoted the sagacious words of Ayn Rand: **"A businessman cannot force you to buy his product; if he makes a mistake, he suffers the consequences; if he fails, he takes the loss. If bureaucrat makes a mistake, you suffer the consequences; if he fails, he passes the loss on to you."**

After Walter finished, receiving a standing ovation, Lori unwaveringly spoke about election corruption and reminded all that Baros's administration had overwhelming evidence.

Father Theodore inquisitively thought to himself: *That is peculiar. Why is there an activated fighterbot in the distance? What is it planning to do?* As Lori was concluding her speech, Father Theodore abruptly shoved his pregnant sister out of the way and took the bullet that was clearly intended for her. The assassin fighterbot used a sophisticated high-power rifle to murder Father Theodore instantly with a deadly shot to his head, which splattered his blood and brains onto his devastated sister. The mortified and aghast audience immediately started screaming and panicking. Security saw and targeted the deadly *fighterbot*. After yelling for everyone to take cover, security opened fire on the robot. The lethal robot was vanquished after ten seconds of fierce fighting and mayhem. Unfortunately, the deadly *fighterbot* murdered sixteen other innocent souls and injured numerous others, including two heroic security guards. These courageous guards' actions exemplified George Orwell's principle: **"We sleep safe in our beds because rough men stand ready in the night to visit violence on those who would do us harm."** A conscientious secret servicewoman, Mrs. Smith, found a *black rose* on the podium. Fortunately, Mrs. Smith knew not to touch it; she informed Walter to confirm that the first family was aware of it.

The stunned and despondent Baros family was kneeling in reverence near their deceased brother; they were in complete mourning. The shocked participants were in complete disbelief and silent. A priest and paramedic came over to assist. The conscientious paramedic instantly realized that Father Theodore had departed, given the devastating damage to his skull; she carefully placed a white sheet over the lifeless body. Lori thought to herself, *God, please allow my brother into your glorious heaven. Please reward my beloved brother for making the ultimate sacrifice.*

The priest from the audience initiated a prayer as the family and others prayed. The priest concluded by reading from Romans 13:4: **"For he is God's servant for your good. But if you do wrong, be afraid, for he does not bear the sword in vain. For he is the servant of God, an avenger who carries out God's wrath on the wrongdoer."**

The priest emotionally expressed, "Father Theodore and I went through seminary together. He was a good friend and devoted priest. I will assist in any way to ease your suffering."

The sorrowful priest, Father Savio, strived to compose himself to support the family. The paramedics respectfully took the body. Walter called his parents and told them the terrible news; his mother collapsed during the phone call. Their mother was immediately rushed to the hospital since they feared that she was having a heart attack. President Baros dashed to the hospital; he remained there with her until she was released the next day. The president purchased two *nursebots* to attend to his wife and family's medical necessities. In addition, he asked Father Savio to assist with her spiritual needs, and he came over to their mansion to comfort her in her grief. Father Savio reminded Li Jing of 1 Thessalonians 4:14: **"For if we believe that Jesus died and rose again, even so them also which sleep in Jesus will God bring with him."**

The biased legacy media attempted to spin this as ultimately President Baros's fault for holding these controversial rallies; the media claimed that the president was spewing misinformation and falsehoods. Ironically, the media failed to report that the security detail was understaffed and not the highly trained secret servicemen that generally accompanied President Baros and his family; they clearly had failed to remove the Baros family immediately when danger was realized. Furthermore, security failed to act on several warnings prior to the assassination of Father Theodore. The bureaucrats' excuse for the security failure was that the secret service had higher priorities, such as the wives of Senator Cain and Carl Flight, who were holding their events at the same time.

Unfortunately, at basically the same time, the Senate agreed to initiate the second dubious impeachment trial in the next few days. Congressman Drakos was performing television and radio interviews to discuss current issues. Congressman Drakos repeatedly stated, "President Baros, without a doubt, is guilty of high crimes and misdemeanors. He should be removed from office without delay and never allowed to hold an elected office again. He is a total disgrace to the presidency." Congressman Drakos began to smear the entire Baros family. He expressed numerous times that Baros had abused his power by questioning a flawless and perfectly executed election. He also said that Baros was guilty of obstruction of Congress; he refused to cease to conduct inflammatory rallies and made false statements about the unblemished election. He reasoned that the last rally had resulted in the death of Baros's son; thus, Baros had the blood of his son on his hands. He expressed that Baros was clearly to blame for everything.

The unaware globalist did not consider that social media and other forms of communication were revealing what actually happened at the last rally, including the failed and inadequate security for the event. Many people who were not supporters of the president thought that the death of Father Theodore should not be politicized; these sympathetic persons understood that no parent should have to bury their child and empathy should be the response. The legacy media even conceded that President Baros's favorability rating was over 65 percent, and over 68 percent believed that the impeachment trial was purely political. Furthermore, over 75 percent thought the impeachment trial was a waste of time. Hopefully, the majority of Americans were aware of historian and philosopher Will Durant's warning: **"The political machine triumphs because it is a united minority acting against a divided majority."**

The presidential administration had another emergency military staff meeting. President Baros stated, "Unfortunately, North Korea has threatened to invade South Korea again. Admiral Sarah Davis, what is the current situation?"

Admiral Davis meticulously portrayed that North Korea was currently threatening to invade South Korea. Major General Gunner informed that North Korea had been conducting military training exercises that were close to the South Korean border; furthermore, North Korea had conducted unsafe and threatening missile tests. In addition, Sergeant Major Nika emphasized that the North Korean military had conducted an underground nuclear test; South Korea threatened to blow North Korea off the map. After the informative meeting, President Baros called the President of North Korea and promised to meet with him and his staff.

The legacy media and globalist party leaders were loudly banging the war drums. These warmongers claimed that North Korea had gone too far, and the only answer was total war. Moreover, they argued that President Baros was a lame-duck president and should not attempt to resolve this. President-elect Cain, soon to be sworn in, should determine what course of action to implement. The legacy media did not understand George

Orwell's warning: **"All the war-propaganda, all the screaming and lies and hatred, comes invariably from people who are not fighting."**

After transporting his beloved wife home and guaranteeing that she received proper care, President Baros flew on the *Baros Express*, Airforce One, to meet with President Kan in Pyongyang, North Korea. President Baros powerfully emphasized that North Korea's actions would not be tolerated and proclaimed that this would be their last belligerent act. However, North Korea preferred to be allies with South Korea and to foster increased commerce and peace.

After an extensive heated conversation and much saber rattling, President Kan declared, "You have not exploited the death of your son, which other world leaders would have done since they are spineless. I am only aware of your personal tragedy from the world news; of course, I am also aware of your opposition party's slanderous smears toward you, which seem to be relentless. You have sincerely expressed your desire to resolve this situation. I had a son assassinated by my enemies; no man should bury their child. Besides, I know that your son, like my son, had a *black rose* near his lifeless body. You and I have a common enemy. I promise you and only you that as long as you are president, I shall guarantee peace with South Korea. Furthermore, I shall give you additional evidence behind the *black rose* and **Mr. Black Rose,** who I am willing to kill with my bare hands. He finances the biolab, an alleged weapons program located in North Korea that the CCP operates. As you are aware, the world's legacy media, based on info from the deep state, have declared that the Doggam pandemic is over. I shall give you evidence that the Doggam pandemic originated from the CCP-controlled biolab and was directed by *Mr. Black Rose*. In regard to your son, I desire this Korean proverb for you and your family: 'At the end of hardship comes happiness.'"

The two headstrong leaders departed after expressing additional kind words along with their goodbyes. On Airforce One, President Baros pondered Luke 23:12: "And the same day Pilate and Herod were made friends together: for before they were at enmity between themselves." Both sides were striving to avoid a Faustian pact.

The legacy media immediately proclaimed that President Baros had caused greater tensions and that he would have blood on his hands; however, on *World News Newsflash*, South Korean President Nam expressed that warring tension with North Korea had decreased significantly and peace should be the ultimate outcome. He thanked President Baros publicly for convening with President Kan. Furthermore, President Kan and he would meet in the future to improve their respective countries' relationship. He expressed the Korean proverb: "You have to measure it to know if it's long or short." In other words, you will never know until you try. As a result of President Nam's gratitude, the legacy media had an egg on its face. President Baros's popularity continued to surge. President Baros understood South African President Nelson Mandela: "If you want to make peace with your enemy, you have to work with your enemy. Then he becomes your partner."

The Baros family was gathering to support their mother; unfortunately, Walter could not attend. Walter was with the coroner to verify the body of his brother, Father Theodore. Li Jing was beginning to feel better; however, she undoubtedly had a heavy heart and a feeling of emptiness. Her entire family was undoubtedly grieving and lamenting; mourners were lighting candles and placing flowers around the White House and Baros Manor. Li Jing was profoundly appreciative and grateful for all the people's support and compassion. In addition, Teresa and Sean gave their loving mother the desirable support and love that she clearly required.

The next day, Walter and Lori were arranging the funeral for their brother as they met with the bishop of the Indianapolis diocese. Bishop Martin expressed his sincere condolences and prayers for their family loss; he greatly respected Father Theodore and was proud to have ordained him as a priest. Furthermore, the bishop agreed that he would perform the funeral and expressed gratitude to the Baros family for their largesse to the church to offset the cost of the funeral, which was expected to be enormous. Bishop Martin reminded the Baros family of Psalm 23:1: **"The LORD is my shepherd; I shall not want."**

A few days later, the Senate was underway with the second impeachment trial of President Baros while the Baros family was burying Father Theodore. Hundreds of priests attended the funeral mass that Bishop Martin conducted. The mass was religiously moving with a remarkably appropriate sermon. Walter and Lori both said words of praise for their brother as President Baros embraced his beloved, teary-eyed wife. Following the mass, the funeral parade left for the final resting place. The funeral procession extended for miles.

At the grave, the bishop eulogized, "Father Theodore is now in heaven with Jesus, since Father Theodore was a faithful servant of the Lord. We must remember that God has preserved Father Theodore's soul. I shall conclude with Father Theodore's favorite Bible verse, Psalm 23:4: **'Even though I walk through the darkest valley, I will fear no evil, for you are with me; your rod and your staff, they comfort me.'"**

The next day, Walter and his sister Lori went to Father Theodore's grave. There, they discovered a dozen *black roses* and a shredded American flag. Lori broke down and cried. Walter comforted his sister and thought, *I shall revenge this act if it is the last thing I do. These bastards are already dead to me.*

At the Senate, the impeachment trial opened with the reading of the three articles of impeachment. The globalist prosecutors claimed that President Baros *abused his power* by questioning the election results, that he was guilty of *obstruction of Congress* for not ceasing to conduct rallies, and that he had *interfered* with the election outcomes. The globalist prosecutors claimed that President Baros was, without a doubt, guilty of all three charges and should be banned from ever holding another governmental office. They claimed that he was a tyrant and that he was wrongly questioning and mocking the obviously impartial and excellent election results; he had only questioned the election results because he did not win. They reminded the jury, the Senate, that the *voterbots* were from Baros's megacorporation, Megadroid; the prosecutors argued that if the *voterbots* were corrupt, then President Baros was responsible since his factories had manufactured them. Furthermore, if the *voterbots* were not corrupt, then President Baros had lied about voting corruption. Thus, either way, President Baros was duplicitous and corrupt. Moreover, the robot that assassinated the president's son was from the same company, and the president should take responsibility for that as well. Since the president was a mechanical engineer and his liability was open to all, the prosecutors reminded everyone of the wise words of former President Herbert Hoover, an engineer: **"The great liability of the engineer compared to men of other professions is that his works are out in the open where all can see them. His acts, step by step, are in hard substance. He cannot bury his mistakes in the grave like the doctors. He cannot argue them into thin air or blame the judge like the lawyers."**

At the questionable impeachment trial, the prosecution presented their so-called evidence. They showed a typical rally and, of course, moderated the event. These globalist prosecutors attempted to demonstrate that President Baros was spewing lies and misinformation about the election. They claimed stubbornly that the president's charisma was fueling civil unrest. Furthermore, the prosecution revealed the timeline of rallies, which clearly violated the congressional cease-and-desist orders. The prosecution claimed that President Baros agreed with Richard Nixon: **"When the President does it, that means that it's not illegal."**

At the White House, the first lady was coping with her family's loss. Sean, with his fiancée Mariana, was comforting his mom. Chef Rosa was preparing a delightful dinner of bao zi (large, hamburger-size dumplings) and rice, Li Jing's ambrosia. President Baros was running late since he was conducting another meeting with his military staff about *Operation Integrity*. *Servicebot Chauffeur* answered the door; Li Jing quickly met Marcus and gave him a loving embrace and kiss. Mega and Max loyally followed Li Jing as their tails were wagging. Marcus stated, "Love, I love you. We shall survive this." Li Jing frightfully thought to herself, *Marcus, I fear that they will assassinate you next.*

Since the Doggam pandemic was declared to be over by government experts, people were beginning to resume their normal lives. Sean and Mariana were watching Teresa's basketball team. The competitive game was extremely exciting and close against a local rival school. With three seconds remaining, Teresa passed the ball to Sofia, who scored the winning basket with an easy layup as she was fouled; Sofia made the free throw, which clinched the game. The duo scored over thirty points. Their team was now 14–0 heading into the annual New Year conference tournament. After the impressive win, Sean took his sister and others out to a well-deserved dinner at his sister's favorite eatery, O'Daddy's Diner, a 1950s-themed hamburger restaurant.

At the delightful café, Teresa stated, "Our brother, Father Teddy, always took me out after a game or when I was feeling down. I truly miss him."

Sean gave her a rosary that their brother had blessed. Teresa embraced Sean and wept. She contemplated 1 Timothy 2:5: **"For there is one God, and one mediator between God and men, the man Christ Jesus…"**

In unexpected rulings, two state supreme courts declared that since President Baros had violated the Fourteenth Amendment by enticing an insurrection and causing a rebellion, any vote cast for him in the 2088 election would be null and void; their reasoning was based on the controversial rallies and violent reactions that had occurred at the Saskatchewan rally. Baros's rallies were judiciously declared an act of rebellion since violence had occurred.

Saskatchewan had a vote margin of only a few thousand votes and was one of the seven states that had flipped at 5:00 a.m. the day after the election. In addition, this was the same state in which Father Theodore was assassinated. However, the other state, Colorado, was not in question, and the president had won by over fifty thousand votes. The Colorado Supreme Court used the same reasoning as the Saskatchewan Supreme Court. In each state, the decision was 4–3; all seven judges in each court were globalist-appointed; however, the judges supporting the decision were all from the ivory towers of elite law schools and funded by *Mr. Black Rose.*

Lori's legal teams immediately appealed the decisions. Moreover, several organizations sued that their rights were violated since their vote would not be counted. It was clearly obvious that lawfare was in full swing. Lori illuminated her father that these courts did not learn from Andrew Jackson's warning: **"All the rights secured to the citizens under the Constitution are worth nothing, and a mere bubble, except guaranteed to them by an independent and virtuous Judiciary."**

As a result of the controversial court rulings, truckers united to boycott two states. They refused to haul goods into Saskatchewan and Colorado. Even though nearly 70 percent of the trucking industry was using autonomous trucks, truck drivers were still used to monitor the self-directed truck convoy. In addition, since 30 percent of trucks were not autonomous, these truckers still had a significant impact on interstate commerce.

These actions caused other economic boycotts from customers and tourists refusing to do business within these states; this was shown by over a 40 percent plunge in e-commerce. This economic boycott was motivated by Martin Luther King Jr.'s words: **"The majority of the Negroes who took part in the year-long boycott of Montgomery's buses were poor and untutored, but they understood the essence of the Montgomery movement; one elderly woman summed it up for the rest. When asked after several weeks of walking whether she was tired, she answered: 'My feet is tired, but my soul is at rest.'"**

6.

THE CORRUPTION
TRIAL

PRIOR TO COUNTING THE ELECTORAL VOTES, Vice President Andrea Argento informed the governors that they must come to Congress, since the Supreme Court had ruled in a 6–3 decision to have a corruption trial for Senator Cain and his running mate, Carl Flight, based on evidence discovered by the military; interestingly, the Supreme Court chief justice did not concur, nor did the other two globalist-appointed justices. One of the added eleven amendments had been executed by the vice president; this anti-Manchurian amendment was created to prevent a fraudulent candidate from becoming president. This modification to the constitution was to prevent a duplicitous candidate from occupying the White House from a corrupt election. It was understood that a fraudulent candidate could theoretically be president due to the court system being judicially deliberate and methodically slow; a Manchurian candidate was not loyal to the country in which they were elected, since their loyalty was to another country or entity that controlled them.

The delay in counting the electoral college votes was due to the presence of alternate electorates in four states and the implementation of the Anti-Manchurian Amendment. Vice President Andrea Argento had executed this decision after reviewing overwhelming evidence from the military, which Sergeant Major Nika recommended. Sergeant Major Nika showed that globalist-controlled states, specifically the seven that claimed they had stopped counting around 10:00 p.m., had cheated in the election by manipulating *voterbots* and allowing ineligible voters to cast their votes to a degree that clearly led to a false result. Interestingly, President Baros did not advise the vice president to take this action. The vice president discovered strong evidence of vote falsification and *voterbot* tampering in several globalist states. Furthermore, the military had evidence linking **Mr. Black Rose** to funding and directing the corruption.

After executing the anti-Manchurian amendment, Congress voted along party lines to impeach the vice president, ultimately creating a constitutional crisis. The vice president was striving to live up to the spirit of Abraham Lincoln's words: **"We the people are the rightful masters of both Congress and the courts, not to overthrow the Constitution but to overthrow the men who pervert the Constitution."**

That evening, Vice President Andrea Argento canceled a trip from his home state to a convention since his wife was not feeling well; she was suffering from the flu. Fatefully, his scheduled plane exploded in mid-flight; this devastating disaster resulted in 234 deaths. What seemed outlandish and awkward was the fact that the legacy media barely covered the airline disaster. The vice president and his family secured a flight back to the Capitol. Prior to leaving, the vice president discovered a *black rose* in the mailbox; he realized that he should not touch it since he had been informed during several intel briefs that *black roses* had a biotoxin. He thought of the words of Robert Kennedy, an assassinated American politician and lawyer: **"What has violence ever accomplished? What has it ever created? No martyr's cause has ever been stilled by an assassin's bullet. No** wrongs have ever been righted by riots and civil disorders. A sniper is only a coward, not a hero; and an uncontrolled or uncontrollable mob is only the voice of madness, not the voice of the people."

Shortly after the vice president and his family left, the FBI raided their home with full force. This dubious search was done without any warning and with an unreadable warrant; the FBI agents wore civilian attire without any identification. The FBI confiscated a plethora of documents and files. Their actions were caught on the home security system. The vice president was able to monitor the entire event. The vice president contacted the head of the FBI for an explanation. The FBI director informed him that the FBI had suspected that there were top-secret documents at his residency.

Vice President Andrea Argento responded, "Even if this is true, why would you raid my home? I would have been extremely cooperative to provide access; I had nothing to hide."

Congressman Drakos called for an emergency House of Representatives vote on articles of impeachment against the vice president. The primary article claimed that the vice president had no constitutional authority to delay the count of the electoral votes and was guilty of not executing his constitutional duties after a fair and legal presidential election.

Ironically, the Senate and House of Representatives could not muster three-fifths of the votes to prevent the vice president from executing the anti-Manchurian amendment and calling for the governors. Congressman Drakos was furious since his bene-factors, like *Mr. Black Rose*, had pressured him to make this go away; however, he did gather enough votes to impeach the vice president. This impeachment trial would start after the conclusion of the president's impeachment trial.

At a secured military staff meeting to discuss *Operation Integrity*, President Baros agreed with the generals' and admirals' recommendations to declare martial law. Major General Gunner explained that the triggering events had occurred. Sergeant Major Nika presented evidence that other globalist nations were involved in the election hoax and were financed by a cabal and ***Mr. Black Rose***. Based on the preponderance of the manifested evidence, the president agreed that rebellion and foreign acts of war were occurring; thus, President Baros instituted martial law. The rebels had metaphorically crossed the Rubicon. Furthermore, Admiral Sarah Davis articulated that the military had the authority to arrest for acts of rebellion and treason on American soil. Martial law was declared to uphold the maxim of Andrew Jackson: **"Disunion by force is treason."**

At the annual girls' basketball conference tournament, Teresa's high school team was in the game. Sean and Mariana attended this exciting barn burner. For the first three quarters, both teams were putting on a clinic, with neither team having any real advantage. However, within the first minute of the fourth period, Teresa swished two three-pointers in a row; in addition, Sofia stole the ball, which resulted in a coast-to-coast layup. The lead was now eight points, which was never challenged again. The victorious squad won 68–56, and the Saint Peter's women's basketball team had an undefeated record of seventeen wins. Mariana became hoarse from cheering and yelling during the blockbuster game. The team was inspired by basketball coach John Wooden's axiom: **"Talent is God-given. Be humble. Fame is man-given. Be grateful. Conceit is self-given. Be careful."**

Sean and Mariana went to an award ceremony after the game. It was a welcome respite where they could eat and bond with their friends. Little did they know the night would end in terror as an assassin attempted to shoot Sean and Mariana. Fortunately, the school's security and their assigned bodyguards and *guardbots* prevented the murderous thug from discharging his weapon. Only a handful of people in the audience were aware of what was happening; they, of course, were stunned and dismayed. However, the lion's share of spectators did not witness the act since law enforcement acted swiftly and prudently, and the arrest occurred outside of the gym near the concession stand. The fortunate news was that Teresa and Sofia were unaware; unfortunately, Sean was completely aware since he saw the assassin near the concession stand prior to his arrest. One of Sean's bodyguards and his *guardbot* escorted Mariana and Sean to a safer location. The other bodyguard stayed with security to protect Teresa and the school. As the bodyguards were patrolling and securing the area, they found two *black roses* with a shredded American flag; a *guardbot* safeguarded the *black roses* as evidence in potential future indictments; interestingly, the *black roses'* toxicity stained the *guardbot's* hands.

As Mariana and Sean arrived at the White House, Li Jing immediately came and embraced them. She was clearly a nervous wreck; fortunately, she had improved at dealing with family tragedies. Mega and Max were excellent at comforting her and giving her a feeling of security since they were exceptional guard dogs.

An hour later, Teresa was still bewildered since her bodyguard had just told her what had happened as they were driving home. When she saw her mother, she embraced her right away and reassured her that everyone was fine; she expressed that they would overcome this. President Baros arrived, thanked the bodyguards, and agreed with them on how to increase security; he agreed to acquire five additional *guardbots*. The president was speechless when they told him of the discovery of two *black roses* with a shredded American flag. The president pondered, *These black roses are a symbol of murder and demise.*

The FBI raided the office of the vice president's personal attorney, Demos Manos, with full battle gear and a redacted warrant, providing no prior notice. Demos was an exceptional friend of the vice president's family and their lawyer for over eighteen years. The questionable search included the attorney's entire law firm.

Demos called the vice president. He expressed, "Andrea, the FBI violated your rights of client-attorney privilege. They took all your files and anything related to you. Moreover, they confiscated all the law firm's computers and other electronic devices! Clearly, our rights and my clients' rights have been violated." The FBI did not learn from Ayn Rand's warning: **"We are fast approaching the stage…where the government is free to do anything it pleases, while the citizens may act only by permission."**

After another day of the impeachment trial, eleven military police officers (MPs) were waiting outside the Senate as the senators departed. The colonel, who was in charge, announced that he had arrest warrants for three globalist senators for conspiring to assassinate and kill Vice President Alfred Jones and conspiring to overthrow the government, which was an act of treason. After reading their rights, the MPs arrested the three accused senators. An arrested senator claimed that he was immune from being arrested since the Senate was in session and the military had no authority to arrest citizens.

The colonel responded, "Sir, the president has declared martial law, which grants us the authority to arrest alleged rebels and traitors." One of the senators who was being arrested pulled out a revolver in an attempt to provoke the police to shoot him, essentially attempting to commit suicide by threatening the police with a deadly weapon. Fortunately, the MPs were able to restrain him immediately, and no shots were fired.

The clearly biased legacy media reported that the military had no authority to arrest any citizen, especially a senator. In addition, the fourth estate claimed that this was probably President Baros's fault since the military was extremely supportive of him; the media claimed that over 80 percent of the military supported Baros; the commentaries claimed that soldiers were just useful idiots for the president. The legacy media proclaimed that this was definitely an act of rebellion, since President Baros would do anything to remain in power. Besides, these three senators would have voted to remove President Baros. The biased media did not acknowledge that martial law had been declared; however, alternate media sources did get the word out. Since the president advocated that the United States was one in sovereignty and protection, martial law was declared and implemented in the spirit of the words of President George Washington: **"But if the laws are to be so trampled upon with impunity, and a minority is to dictate to the majority, there is an end put at one stroke to republican government, and nothing but anarchy and confusion is to be expected thereafter."**

Congress was advocating for another one-hundred-billion-dollar aid bill to support the separatists against the Argentinian government. Tension with the separatists was snowballing with increased fighting and chaos; they were clearly at war. President Baros did not want to get involved; besides, he was convinced that a significant portion of this aid would just be returned to the politicians; however, he knew that he must do something.

President Baros arranged to meet with the president of Argentina to reduce tensions. After flying the *Baros Express* to the Argentina summit, he expressed that he had no desire to interfere. However, he had no desire for this situation to escalate; he understood that this was an internal problem. He encouraged President Carlos Fernadez to work with the separatists. Carlos stated that the problem was that the American money intended for lithium mine workers was never received. He was willing to work with the United States in order to guarantee that the workers were paid. Carlos required assistance to reduce corruption. Carlos explained that **Mr. Black Rose** was probably behind the corruption, since he and his cabal were against Argentina being a Nationalist country. President Baros assured Carlos that the US military would ensure that the lithium mine workers were paid, including back pay, since this was already congressionally authorized. President Baros adhered to President John F. Kennedy's statement: **"Let us never negotiate out of fear. But let us never fear to negotiate."**

Sean and Mariana were watching her sister's basketball team again, which was currently undefeated. They were playing a rival, which was the largest high school in the state and had ten times the enrollment of Teresa's high school. This team had won the state championship last year. After three quarters, the two teams were even at 48–48. With only thirty-three seconds to go, the two teams were still knotted at 64–64. The opposing team had the ball. Teresa pickpocketed the ball and shot for a deep two: nothing but net. Next, the opposing team came down the court and heaved a three-pointer bank shot at the last second. Teresa's team suffered their first loss; they were now 17–1. Teresa remembered that when her team lost their first game last year, Father Theodore had jokingly expressed a quote by Vince Lombardi, Green Bay Packers coach: **"Show me a good loser, and I'll show you a loser."** He then stated that he disagreed with this quote and believed her performance and effort truly embodied the true spirit of sportsmanship.

Vice President Andrea Argento was in the senate chambers to welcome the sixty-two governors who would be jurors for the corruption trial. Currently, forty-five governors were nationalists; however, two governors were allegedly being blackmailed by the deep state. They were known to have visited and vacationed at Make-Believe Island. Since Supreme Court Justice Johnathon Robertson was conducting the impeachment trial of President Baros and potentially the impeachment trial of the vice president, Senior Justice Tony Romano would conduct the trial; he had been appointed by a nationalist president in 2070. He was well-known for believing in a strict reading of the Constitution and opposed an activist's judicial interpretation. Justice Tony Romano was a disciple of Supreme Court Justice Antonin Scalia, who said: **"If you're going to be a good and faithful judge, you have to resign yourself to the fact that you're not always going to like the conclusions you reach. If you like them all the time, you're probably doing something wrong."**

The House of Representatives determined who would be the acting president starting on January 20, 2089, as the anti-Manchurian amendment was activated. Each state had only one vote regardless of the number of representatives. Since the nationalists had nearly 70 percent of the states, President Baros would remain president and be sworn in as the acting president on January 20. However, the acting president status was effective, at most, until May 1. Justice Tony Romano ordered that all governors report to DC, Kansas, as jurors for the corruption trial, which would start on January 24. He told the defense and prosecution to prepare for the upcoming trial of Senator John Cain and his running mate, Carl Flight. This judicial format was the first of its kind; however,

this prosecution arrangement was clearly similar to an impeachment trial format. In order to fulfill the anti-Manchurian amendment, Supreme Court Justice Tony Romano ordered the military
to conduct another presidential election within sixty days. The
results would only be relevant if Senator John Cain were found
guilty, since the previous election would be null and void. This
admittedly was considered controversial by some legal scholars;
however, all agreed that once the Supreme Court accepted the
anti-Manchurian amendment, the complete constitutional process must occur, including a military-run alternate election.

During the impeachment trial, the prosecution had rested.
The defense began to bring witnesses after opening remarks. The
first witness, who was an expert on constitutional law, said that
the president was correct not to listen to Congress due to the
separation of powers and checks and balances. The president had
no constitutional duty to cease and desist at the will of Congress.
They brought other witnesses to express that he did not abuse his
powers or interfere with the elections. One witness illuminated
that the president had a duty to ensure that elections were performed legally and fairly, whether he benefitted or not.

The defense attempted to enter evidence from the military
about election corruption. The chief justice blocked the evidence
from being entered since he believed that this evidence was clearly
speculative and dubious. The military evidence revealed that the
voterbots were tampered with, and voter fraud occurred when
the so-called precincts claimed to have stopped counting votes;
in addition, there was significant other damning evidence. The
defense adamantly disagreed; however, the chief justice did not
change his ruling. After both sides concluded with their closing

arguments, the chief justice instructed the Senate to vote. The vote was 114-69 in favor to acquit; the president was found not guilty.

On a tranquil, gorgeous halcyon day in Kansas, January 20, President Baros was sworn in as the acting president of the United States by Justice Tony Romano. Li Jing was there to support her husband. Acting President Baros reflected to himself, *I must heed the warning of Abraham Lincoln's words: "**America will never be destroyed from the outside. If we falter and lose our freedoms, it will be because we destroyed ourselves.**"*

The legacy media was livid and suffering from a complete meltdown; some were claiming that democracy was dead. They adamantly maintained that the impeachment trial went merely along party lines; the nationalists would ultimately never remove one of their own. In addition, the vice president created a constitutional crisis by calling for the governors and voting for a presidential corruption trial for the first time in history; the legacy media insisted that there was no evidence of any election corruption. They advocated that the current administration was willing to do anything to remain in power; this corrupt administration was a tyrannical dictatorship and may cause a civil war. One commentator emphatically proclaimed, "Der Führer Baros is a despotic evil NAZI!"

The biased legacy media was surprised that the president was still gaining support and popularity; they did not understand the adverse effect of the Supreme Court chief justice denying the military's right to enter evidence into the trial; the populace generally believed that the military was the least politically biased governmental entity. Alternate media sources, such as the internet and podcasts, ensured that the people were informed properly and accurately, or at least revealed an alternate viewpoint. The populace had a positive perspective of the military since they generally agreed with the sentiment of Gilbert K. Chesterton, an English author: **"The true soldier fights not because he hates what is in front of him, but because he loves what is behind him."**

The active military, under Admiral Sarah Davis, with the assistance of the National Guard, was preparing to conduct a presidential election, which would only be valid if Senator Cain and his vice presidential candidate were convicted. The election would be between acting president Baros of the nationalist party and Congressman Drakos of the globalist party; Drakos's name was there in case Senator Cain and running mate Carl Flight were convicted. The military activated National Guard units in all sixty-two states to oversee and preserve the presidential election. The election would be conducted on one day with paper ballots. Unfortunately, if a person was in a foreign country on the day of the election, then this person must vote at an American embassy or United States military base in that country. All voters had to show a valid national ID, obtainable at most federal buildings and post offices. This election was scheduled for Saint Patrick's Day 2089. The goal of the military was to adhere to the words of President George H. W. Bush: **"We know what works: freedom works. We know what's right: freedom is right. We know how to secure a more and just and prosperous life for man on**

Earth: through free markets, free speech, free elections, and the exercise of free will unhampered by the state."

Throughout the globalist-controlled states, especially enormous metropolitan cities, there were many organized protests against President Baros as an interim president; unfortunately, in a majority of circumstances, there was rioting, pillaging, and rebelling; the military suspected that a secret group of benefactors financially funded the protestors. The alias name of *Mr. Black Rose* was being whispered among the military investigators; there was a short list of people who might be *Mr. Black Rose*. Suspiciously, the coldhearted *policebots* were not arresting or engaging violent protestors or rioters except in nationalist-controlled areas. Since martial law had been declared, the National Guard was mobilized to constrain the situation. Over 70 percent of the country supported the efforts of the National Guard. They understood the words of George Washington: **"When we assumed the Soldier, we did not lay aside the Citizen."**

The globalist governors refused to recognize the orders from Admiral Sarah Davis and the acting president. Admiral Davis, with the president's approval, federalized the National Guard units within these rebellious globalist states as well as essential units in nationalist-controlled states. Rebel *policebots* manufactured by other robotic companies and funded by *Mr. Black Rose* and the cabal were attacking National Guard soldiers and their *fighterbots* within these defiant states and cities; the rebel *policebots* were under the direct orders of their state's commander and chief and generals.

Three governors and their respective state generals were arrested by the military police. Prior to their arrests, these three governors were advocating for civil war and rebellion. Since the governors were recognized as the commanders in chief of their states, they were treated as enemy combatants as well as traitors. In addition, at one of the governor's homes, the MPs fortuitously discovered a notebook with individual names of people who allegedly worked for **Mr. Black Rose** and who were devout supporters of secular globalutopianism, de-Christianization, and anti-traditional family values. The military adhered to the principle of Corneliu Zelea Codreanu, a Romanian politician: **"The first and fiercest punishment ought to fall first on the traitor, second on the enemy. If I had but one bullet and I were faced by both an enemy and a traitor, I would let the traitor have it."**

At the White House, the Baros extended family was meeting. Teresa was ecstatic that her adept basketball team had rebounded from their first loss by slaughtering their local Catholic rival; the duo, Teresa and Sofia, had combined scores and assists of forty-eight and twenty, respectively; after emptying the bench, the substitute players played the entire fourth quarter; the lopsided final score was 94–38. Furthermore, their team won the next two games easily; the impressive girls' basketball team was now 20–1, and they were the girls' basketball conference champion for the second year in a row. The sectional was starting next week.

After the game, Rex asked Sofia to go to prom with him. She teasingly responded, "Let me think about it." Sofia did not want to reveal that she thought that Rex was a charming Adonis; in addition, she did not want to come across as frantic.

Sean chimed in that baseball was going well, and their team was three and one. Next, Rex mentioned that their chess team had won the 2089 annual Indianapolis High School chess tournament for the second year in a row. The Golden Knights were still undefeated with seven wins. Rex reflected on Bobby Fischer's saying: **"A strong memory, concentration, imagination, and a strong will is required to become a great chess player."**

The televised corruption trial triggered by the anti-Manchurian amendment was in session, with Supreme Court Justice Tony Romano and the sixty-two governors who represented each of their respective states as jurors. The honorable judge expressed, before opening remarks from each side, that his goal was to complete this trial one week before the required presidential elections on Saint Patrick's Day; however, the rights of the defendant and due process would be paramount. The prosecution began by expressing that the presidential election was fraudulent. They presented evidence that would demonstrate that President Baros won and all votes tabulated after 10:00 p.m. were illegal and fraudulent. The defense stated that this entire case against Senator Cain and Carl Flight was a complete farce; Senator Cain should have been sworn in as the president. As a result of not executing the lawful November election, the defense vigorously argued that the voters and electorates had been disenfranchised when their votes were illegally disqualified.

President Baros and his legal team were discussing legal strategies. One lawyer stated that the prosecution would introduce their evidence in a couple of days regarding the corruption trial. President Baros stated, "I am extremely delighted that the Honorable Supreme Court Justice Romano allowed the corruption trial to be televised; this should prevent the mainstream media from spinning the evidence and final verdict."

In February of 2089, Sean and Mariana brought his mom to watch the final game of the sectional. The family knew that their mother should get out; they were striving to cheer her up. She was feeling better about her family attending since security had been increased with several *guardbots*, security guards, and secret servicemen. At the game, Li Jing enjoyably cheered for her daughter's impressive team. The game was never in question since Saint Peter Catholic High School took an early lead and never looked back; it was another blowout. The victorious team was now 23–1 and heading to the regional games for the third year in a row; however, the Saint Peter Catholic High School girls' basketball team had ended the season at the regional game last year. Li Jing was tremendously proud of Teresa and Sofia since they each scored over twenty points and had over ten assists, a double-double.

During February and expectedly March, the military imposed a nationwide curfew under martial law from 9:00 p.m. to 6:00 a.m., allowing some normalcy during the day. However, the military and police ruled the night. Fortunately, during the day, schools and businesses were open, with the ominous reality of a military presence. *Servicebot Educator* was delighted since he would not need to assist Rex and Teresa as much. The excellent news for Teresa, Rex, and Sean was that their respective schools had no interruptions to their learning or academic and athletic programs in February and March; at this time, Sean and Rex should be able to graduate on time, and they were expected to be able to play baseball; in addition, Rex still planned to finish his senior year with a great lacrosse season.

Li Jing celebrated the Chinese New Year with her entire family on February 10, 2089, the Chinese Year of the Rooster. They all went into the holograph room and enjoyed a simulated Chinese fireworks show as they ate several Chinese delicacies prepared by Chef Rosa with the assistance of *Servicebot Cook*; when the spectacular and spellbinding fireworks were completed, the simulation illuminated a plethora of cherry blossom trees blooming. Li Jing reminded her family of Confucius's maxim: **"To put the world in order, we must first put the nation in order; to put the nation in order, we must first put the family in order; to put the family in order, we must first cultivate our personal life; and to cultivate our personal life, we must first set our hearts right."**

During the corruption trial, the prosecution's first witness described the suspicious timeline on election day. The witness emphasized that President Baros was in the lead at 10:00 p.m. She stated that seven states claimed that they still needed to complete tabulating all their respective votes; they were not finished. Furthermore, she expressed that all seven states had at least one major metropolitan precinct close at 10:00 p.m. All precincts reported that no more counting would occur until 5:00 a.m.

The second witness, who was an expert on historical voting trends and statistical analysis, verified that the Globalist Party heavily ruled all these closed precincts; historically, over 70 percent of voters in those precincts voted for globalist candidates. Moreover, this expert witness said that all these precincts had more votes cast than the number of eligible voters in the precincts, from at least 7 percent more to as high as 18 percent. President Baros would have won all seven states if the votes counted after 10:00 p.m. were removed. Additionally, he rationalized that statistically and scientifically, with two hours left, President Baros had over a 99.999 percent chance of winning; in other words, his chances of losing were basically one in a hundred thousand.

The third witness was a military intelligence officer, a major, within the space force. The space force had monitored activities within all the allegedly closed precincts. The videos demonstrated that counting had continued, and the *voterbots* had still been sending vote counts electronically while they were secured in the precincts and clearly not gathering additional votes; all these precincts had been closed to the public. Furthermore, videos showed the *voterbots* being tampered with in order to increase the voting count and adjust the time stamp of votes to before 6:00 p.m. on election day.

The fourth military witness was another military intelligence officer, a colonel, who educated the jury about ballot watermarks, which accounted for approximately 25 percent of the votes. She enlightened the jury and the judge on some key points. First, over 10 percent of the ballots had a verifiable watermark that was difficult to detect and duplicate; in addition, these watermarked ballots were traceable with location and verification. Second, over 50 percent of watermarked ballots in globalist-controlled precincts came from spurious addresses or non-residential locations. There was overwhelming evidence that over 45 percent of the watermarked ballots in globalist-controlled precincts were cast by non-verifiable persons or those not legally allowed to vote. Third, a few watermarked ballots were illegally duplicated to produce tens of thousands of forgeries.

The evidence of these military witnesses was extremely convincing and overwhelming; the defense was clearly back on its heels. Eight other military witnesses verified these intelligence officers' statements with augmented evidence; several governors' faces blushed red, and they shook their heads with anger. One of the jurors, a nationalist governor, thought to himself about Saint Augustine's words: **"In the absence of justice, what is sovereignty but organized robbery?"**

The thirteenth witness, who was an expert on data verification, expressed that all votes cast in these precincts were from individuals who had resided in these jurisdictions at some point in their lives; however, over 30 percent of them either were dead, had moved out of the precinct, were non-US-citizens, or were criminally ineligible prior to election day. Furthermore, the lion's share of ineligible voters voted late on election day or early the next morning. This indicated that the unqualified or fraudulent votes were utilized only when the criminals had clearly demanded the disqualified votes in order to steal the election.

Three more witnesses, who were whistleblowers and under witness protection, testified that they witnessed nefarious acts by both Senator Cain and his running mate. They observed Senator Cain and Carl Flight orchestrating others to tamper with the *voterbots* and create copied ballots with their names and the names of other loyal globalists pre-marked. Two witnesses stated that Senator Cain often expressed disregard for election laws and was willing to do whatever it took to win. However, they admitted that they had not heard Carl Flight say this. Many governors thought of the infamous words of Joseph Stalin: **"It's not the people who vote that count. It's the people who count the votes."**

The Saint Peter Catholic High School girls' basketball team won their first regional game in the morning. Unfortunately, that evening they were playing the same state-champion team that had beat them last year in the regional finals; however, on a positive point, practically the entire Saint Peter student body and their families were there. The cheerleaders and their school's mascot, the Golden Knight, were entertaining the fans.

After three nail-biting quarters, the Saint Peter Golden Knights were losing by three points. With thirty-eight seconds left in the fourth quarter, Sofia swished a deep three-pointer, which gave the Golden Knights their first lead. After the opposing team shot the ball, Teresa rebounded the ball, forcing the opposing team to foul as she was attempting a three-point shot, which she air-balled. Teresa made all three free throws, which meant the Golden Knights were ahead by five points with seventeen seconds left. As the buzzer went off, the opposing team threw up a hopeless brick; the Golden Knights fans rushed the basketball court. The announcer declared the Golden Knights as 3A regional girls' basketball champions; the court was a sea of red and gold apparel.

After the game, Sofia saw Rex, who was clearly cheering for her and the team. She delightfully smiled and stated, "Yes, I will go to the prom with you. You should wear a light-blue tuxedo to match my sapphire dress. In addition, I admire red roses, and we will eat a Mexican dinner before the prom." They were both striving to avoid making any faux pas while showing their infatuation with each other.

The following week, unfortunately, the Golden Knights lost in the semi-state finals to the eventual state champions. The Golden Knights girls' basketball team ended their outstanding season with a 25–2 record. Rex consoled Sofia, took her to a glamorous Mexican restaurant, and bestowed her with a dozen red roses; she was extremely grateful. Sofia was impressed with Rex's maturity and absence of any sophomoric behavior or inappropriate innuendos on their first date.

Back at the corruption trial, the defense advocated that the evidence brought forth did not prove corruption. In addition, the defense argued that even if the evidence was true, the prosecution did not show that Senator Cain orchestrated the corruption. Furthermore, the defense claimed that the whistleblowers were lying and that they were non-supporters of Senator Cain, even though the whistleblowers were registered globalists. Moreover, the defense advocated that the military were just President Baros's supporters and would say anything for him. The media were fulfilling the words of Marcus Tullius Cicero: **"When you have no basis for an argument, abuse the plaintiff."**

The military police arrested twelve globalist governors; the arrest warrant stated that they were charged with treason and corruption, and the defendants would stand trial in a military tribunal. Cabal benefactors and *Mr. Black Rose* supported all twelve arrested governors. Immediately, Honorable Supreme Court Justice Romano ruled that the remaining fifty governors would determine the trial outcome, and the other twelve governors would not be replaced. Honorable Supreme Court Justice Romano instructed the fifty governor-jurors to determine whether Senator Cain was guilty or not guilty of election corruption.

After twenty-four hours of deliberations and fierce debates with yelling and screaming, the governor-jurors contacted the judge and said that they were ready to reveal their decision. Honorable Supreme Court Justice Romano entered the courtroom and ordered the jurors to reveal how they voted. The governors voted 42–8 to convict Senator Cain and his running mate and 40–10 to ban them both from holding office again. This decision was determined prior to the military-conducted election on Saint Patrick's Day.

The shocked legacy media was livid and pretentiously arguing against the results of the corruption trial; they advocated that the governors and the military were undoubtedly dishonest. If the military had not interfered, Senator Cain would not have been found guilty. The media repeatedly claimed that not-my-president Baros was a tyrant and was willing to do anything to remain in power. The media, from their ivory towers, seemed to be supporting the violent protests that were happening in globalist-controlled cities; the violence included arson, looting, and murder. The National Guard had additional soldiers called up by nationalist governors who had civil disturbances and riots within their state.

Chief Justice Johnathon Robertson, with the Senate, then started the impeachment trial against the vice president for causing a constitutional crisis. Even the legacy media agreed that this was basically a waste of time, since the nationalist party controlled the Senate. Even the House of Representatives, which was now under the rule of the Nationalist Party, was striving to dismiss the impeachment trial.

The military executed and spearheaded *Operation Anti-Trafficking* under the command of Major General Gunner with his Sergeant Major Kevin Nika. This well-executed operation with exceptional command and control (C2) included invading Make-Believe Island; prior to the attack, cyber warfare and electronic warfare

(EW) were implemented to deceive the enemy. These advanced weapons interrupted all communication on the island. This mission was perilous since the island was well-fortified and well-armed. This dangerous military mission resulted in the arrest of 198 alleged pedophiles on the island; however, they were not able to capture or arrest *Mr. Black Rose*. In addition, sixty-six individuals unfortunately decided to fight and challenge the military. Sergeant Major Nika, with the assistance of the special forces and Navy SEALs, easily took out all sixty-six; unfortunately, the combatants' bodies were damaged to the point of being difficult to identify.

Hardcore Sergeant Major Nika stated to General Gunner, "Sir, *veni, vidi, vici!* We invaded, we targeted, and we pulverized." The great news was that over 288 underage girls and boys were rescued. Furthermore, the military safeguarded the evidence for future convictions.

Major General Gunner grinned and stated, "Hooah!"

The military raid with superior firepower was extremely fruitful since the military detectives discovered videos, DNA evidence, and documentation to indict hundreds of elites throughout the country and the world. Furthermore, they discovered evidence of who was funding and supporting the *plandemic*: the cabal and *Mr. Black Rose*. The alleged elites included politicians, entertainers, CEOs, commentators, and others. In addition, the investigators discovered a notebook called *Black Roses*, which included a list of individuals who were allegedly killed or assassinated, such as Vice President Alfred Jones. Moreover, investigators discovered evidence that the corrupt FBI raid of the vice president was conducted to plant top-secret documents at his home and included shoot-to-kill orders if the vice president had been present. Major

General Gunner's unit's victory was based on his adherence to Samurai Miyamoto Musashi's teaching: **"True warriors are fierce because their training is fierce."**

The military brought additional personnel to the island in order to convert the island into a military base; however, Make-Believe Island's location, edifices, and tunnels were secured in order to gather additional evidence. The new military base would serve as a military prison and location for future military tribunals and executions of prisoners convicted of capital crimes.

On Saint Patrick's Day of 2089, the military conducted the new election throughout the country. There were no *voterbots*, and there was only one day of voting; all voting was done with paper ballots. In each time zone, the elections were conducted from 6:00 a.m. to 6:00 p.m. All voters were required to vote in person with an approved ID; however, in some special circumstances, the military went to the residence of individuals who requested early voting and proved that they were not able to leave their homes.

Unfortunately, there was rioting and disorderly activities in globalist-controlled precincts. That evening, the election results were revealed. President-Elect Baros won in a landslide in the electoral college, 758-220. Furthermore, he won the popular vote by over eight million votes. A few days after the election results were tabulated and the vice president had counted the electoral votes, senior Justice Tony Romano swore Acting President Baros in as the president for his second term. President Baros reflected on President Andrew Jackson's adage: **"If you always support the correct principles then you will never get the wrong results!"**

7.

OPERATION
JUDGMENT DAY

LORI AND HER HUSBAND WALTER were at the hospital. As President Baros and his wife Li Jing arrived, Lori's doctor delivered a healthy baby boy. Walter immediately announced that Lori and he had decided to name the boy Theodore; obviously, they wanted to honor her brother, Father Theodore. The baby Theodore was officially born on March 20, 2089. Marcus and Li Jing were definitely proud grandparents. Marcus reflected on Proverbs 17:6: **"Children's children are the crown of old men; and the glory of children are their fathers."**

The legacy media was in complete meltdown; they were clearly enraged and fuming about President Baros's victory. The activist media were advocating for continued civil unrest and riots. Surprisingly, the military arrested several media commentators while they were broadcasting. These commentators were all alleged visitors to Make-Believe Island and had committed pedophile illegalities as well as other high crimes.

The military presided over and occupied the legacy media broadcasting stations. The military posted servicemen in the broadcasting stations to reveal the truth to the people. First, the military revealed that martial law had been declared throughout the country; the National Guard was mobilized in every state in order to maintain law and order. Second, they emphasized that the military-conducted election was legitimate and warranted; the goal was to guarantee that election laws were executed without the threat of tyranny and corruption. Third, they broadcasted the evidence that was entered in the corruption trial; the military wanted to inform United States citizens of widespread corruption. Fourth, they stated that numerous alleged pedophiles and criminals should be arrested and tried under a military tribunal; the accused were charged with treason, bribery, espionage, national security offenses, pedophilia, and other high crimes.

After a few days, Chief Justice Johnathon Robertson, Senator Cain, Congressman Dillon Drakos, DA Jerome Williams, Judge Richard Pilot, and several other key globalists were arrested by the military, which was also broadcast on various networks. The raids were televised in a few instances. However, these arrests were synchronized to avoid alerting any suspects.

Ironically, Justice Romano immediately ruled that the impeachment trial of Vice President Andrea Argento, after a quick vote from the senators, was dismissed.

The military broadcasters informed the public that a cabal had orchestrated the Doggam pandemic, and the Doggam virus had been developed in North Korea as part of a CCP weapons program.

Admiral Sarah Davis expressed that martial law would not be the norm; the goal was to quickly restore governmental control to the proper authorities and lawfully elected governmental officials. This would occur after allegedly treasonous individuals were arrested; all military-arrested individuals would be held for their crimes and tried in a military tribunal.

Admiral Sarah Davis promised that the constitution would not be violated, especially the Third Amendment: **"No soldier shall, in time of peace, be quartered in any house, without the** consent of the owner, nor in time of war, but in a manner to be prescribed by law." She clearly included the Fourth Amendment: "The right of the people to be secure in their persons, houses, papers, and effects, against unreasonable searches and seizures, shall not be violated, and no warrants shall issue, but upon probable cause, supported by oath or affirmation, and particularly describing the place to be searched and the persons or things to be seized."

Admiral Davis ordered the *Stoic Slayers Task Force* to conduct *Operation Judgment Day*, which was divided into three phases. Major General Gunner would be the commanding general of the *Stoic Slayers Task Force*, an enhanced division. Thirty-year seasoned Sergeant Major Kevin Nika would be his right-hand man. Phase one would eradicate or capture the vital rebel lieutenants within the country, who were the operational and strategic leaders who executed the enemy's command, suspected to be the globalist cabal and *Mr. Black Rose*. Phase one would end when the rebel lieutenants were all eliminated or mission-incapable; all captured rebel lieutenants, after receiving any required medical care, would be sent to the military prison and tribunal courthouse on Make-Believe Island. The captured rebels would be tried and imprisoned on Make-Believe Island.

In phase two the task force would capture, occupy, or remove the rebel command and commander. This phase would end when the rebel's head—suspected to be *Mr. Black Rose*—was removed or dead.

Phase three would eliminate or capture all rebel bases to ensure that they were under friendly forces' control. This phase would end when Divisional Commander Major General Gunner informed Admiral Davis that *Operation Judgment Day* was complete, and she concurred. General Gunner was a disciple of General George Patton, and he agreed with his war objective: **"The object of war is not to die for your country but to make the other bastard die for his."**

During one of the military raids ordered by Major General Gunner as part of phase one, a special forces unit with augmented military police stormed Progressiveville City Hall. Unfortunately, the suspects were prepared. *Fighterbots* entered City Hall and were immediately attacked by the globalist-controlled rebel *policebots*. A special forces officer, Lieutenant Jefferson, armed with a *LAW rocket*, took aim at the rebels. With one lethal launch, he eliminated six rebel *policebots*; unfortunately, the lieutenant was hit by small-arms fire. Luckily, two *fighterbots* instantly shielded him and removed him from danger.

After the *fighterbots* defeated the rebel *policebots*, the rebels set off an explosive at City Hall, killing all globalist suspects and a couple of *fighterbots*. The rebels detonated the bomb because they believed they were being overrun. Sergeant Major Kevin Nika and military police identified the four deceased globalist suspects; they discovered additional evidence and a couple of boxes of *black roses*. So far, all *black roses* obtained were toxic.

The real threat to the military was clearly the fact that numerous criminal globalists were willing to commit suicide in an attempt to take as many friendly forces with them as possible. Fortunately, Lieutenant Jefferson recovered from being shot in the leg, and no other military personnel were injured or killed; Major General Gunner awarded the lieutenant with a well-deserved medal and a purple heart for his heroism. Lieutenant Jefferson reflected on Joel 3:9: **"Proclaim ye this among the Gentiles: Prepare war, wake up the mighty men, let all the men of war draw near; let them come up."**

On the last Wednesday of March, the Saint Daniel's Roaring Lions baseball team commenced their thirtieth game of the season; the coach was searching for his third Division 2 college baseball championship in his thirteenth season. Sean, a southpaw, pitched; his fastball and changeup were blowing the batters away. Before the ace reliever came in, he completed five innings, allowed only three hits and two walks, and struck out eight batters. In addition, he hit two singles and had one RBI as a result of a solo upper-decker home run. The Roaring Lions won 5–1 and had a 24–6 record. This was the last game prior to the country's military lockdown. Little did Sean know that this might be his last game before graduating from college.

Unfortunately, Rex and his baseball team were only 3–0 before the military lockdowns. However, at the last baseball game in March, Saint Peter Catholic High School dedicated the game to Father Theodore. The school honored Father Theodore's baseball performance and teaching by establishing a baseball scholarship in his name. President Baros secretly donated thirty million dollars to the foundation. In addition, Rex and his lacrosse team were on hold as well. Rex was the goalie and allowed less than six goals per game, and he averaged over twelve saves. The lacrosse team was undefeated with four wins; Rex was the best goalie in the state.

Teresa and Sofia were cheerleaders for the lacrosse team. However, Teresa, Sophia, and Rex were concerned that their high school year could be ruined, which included the prom and Rex's high school graduation. All three adored their high school extra-curricular activities and their friends.

Starting March 28, 2089, and during the month of April, the country was under total martial law and military lockdown. Admiral Sarah Davis chose Major General Gunner as the commanding general to spearhead the upcoming military operations; he was a towering and intimidating man who demanded complete adherence to military protocol and discipline. The schools were closed, and the streets were empty. Friendly *policebots* and the military patrolled while over 80 percent of schools were able to conduct online learning. This was misleading, as national-ist-controlled states were practically at 100 percent and globalist states were under 50 percent. For Sean, Rex, and Teresa, in April their respective schools had online learning, which meant that Sean and Rex should be able to graduate on time; however, their extracurriculars were on hold.

Furthermore, Mariana and Sean were planning their marriage in July, which they understood could be delayed; however, they were depressed by this possibility. They felt that their college days were being ruined and feared that their wedding may be delayed for a long time.

On Good Friday of 2089, which was also April Fools' Day, President Baros addressed the nation. He passionately asserted, "United States citizens, who are all divine, sovereign individuals, have been blessed by God with ordained and sacred rights that no government, deep state, or bureaucrat has the right to suspend or take away. Rights are from God and not from the government. The purpose of the United States Constitution is to limit the federal government; the purpose is not to limit the people; the government is for the people, people are not for the government. Furthermore, every citizen has the right to protest and speak against their government and officials peaceably; however, no one has the right to overthrow a government in order to install a globalist dictatorship."

President Baros reiterated his oath of office under Article II, Section 1 of the US Constitution: **"I do solemnly swear (or affirm) that I will faithfully execute the office of President of the United States, and will to the best of my ability, preserve, protect and defend the Constitution of the United States."** He reminded everyone of the Bill of Rights and articles of the Constitution. He acknowledged that the country was under total martial law due to rebels who were actively attempting to overthrow the country; He explained citizens' God-given rights within the First Amendment: **"Congress shall make no law respecting an establishment of religion, or prohibiting the free exercise thereof; or abridging the freedom of speech, or of the press; or the right of the people peaceably to assemble, and to petition the government for a redress of grievances."** He did the same for the Second Amendment: **"...the right of the people to keep and bear arms, shall not be infringed."** He educated the citizens on the United States' civic and government purposes. He assured that martial law would not be prolonged unnecessarily; however, he refrained from promising an end date to avoid aiding the enemy. He informed the nation that twelve globalist-controlled states had declared their secession from the United States. President Baros echoed the wise words of Ayn Rand: **"The government was set to protect man from criminals—and the constitution was written to protect man from the government. The Bill of Rights was not directed at private citizens, but against the government—as an explicit declaration that individual rights supersede any public or social power."**

At Make-Believe Island, the military had built a holding area for the arrested suspects. Originally, the military targeted over one thousand suspects, and the lion's share of suspects were named in the *Black Rose* notebooks. Unfortunately, 316 were killed prior to arrest via suicide or by military police in lawful self-defense. Furthermore, military JAG officers and military lawyers were negotiating with some suspects in order to exchange reduced sentencing for testimony on others, especially evidence against the treasonous ring leaders, like *Mr. Black Rose*. Regrettably, forty-six suspects took their lives within the holding area. A graveyard was established for prisoners that were executed or had died on the island. The graveyard was called Traitorville Last Estate.

Make-Believe Island was one of the smaller tropical islands within the Hawaiian archipelago. There was a grand amusement park and an impressive water park, with a volcano seen in the distance; the landscape was teeming with exotic flora. The MPs found an elaborate, well-maintained greenhouse that grew exotic, picturesque plants, which, of course, included poisonous *black roses*. The main hotel resembled a fantasy castle, with over four hundred bedrooms with hidden entrances; there was a tunnel system that led to rooms used for the exploitation of children or young teenagers; the tunnels were a clandestine labyrinth. At night, the infamous castle was lit with flamboyant lighting. When the grandiose park was in operation at night, the tropical island was lit up with drones and captivating fireworks.

Interestingly, the military had built a military base with a holding area for suspects waiting for trial, as well as a military prison. Eight tribunal courts were constructed to try the defendant in a timely manner. The military focused on functionality and avoided building any gaudy features or structures. Fortunately, the island had a small well-maintained airport with a few helipads and the capability to land large commercial passenger planes. The navy surrounded the island with an armada of battleships, a few aircraft carriers, and stingray submarines; stingray submarines were stealth nuclear-powered high-speed submarines. The impressive air force and space force secured the sky. This military buildup seemed to be beyond the pale; however, rebel globalists regularly attempted to invade the island to free the prisoners.

In Progressiveville, the dedicated National Guard soldiers and *fighterbots* were fighting block by block against anarchist globalist rebels and *policebots*; this was just one example of the fierce battles occurring throughout the country and the world. Lieutenant Jefferson was leading his platoon, the Liberators, against the enemy, with the understanding that the military must protect noncombatants and citizens.

Three rebel *policebots* were performing a summary execution of four young women; the Liberators immediately eliminated the rebel *policebots* without harming the women. The women were instantly sent to the secured rear for medical and social services.

Unfortunately, four additional rebel *policebots* engaged the Liberators. The Liberators were victorious; however, two *fighterbots* were severely damaged, and Sergeant Major Kevin Nika, who gallantly eliminated two deadly rebel *policebots*, was injured with a minor flesh wound. He was quickly sent to the rear, where he was expected to have a full recovery. Sergeant Major Kevin Nika agreed with Samurai Miyamoto Musashi: **"The only reason a warrior is alive is to fight, and the only reason a warrior fights is to win."**

The military executed *Operation Removal*. The special forces, Rangers, and Navy SEALs implemented this joint operation. On the day after April Fools' Day, three simultaneous synchronized missions to remove three suspected globalist rebel governors occurred. The special forces removed traitorous governors from Saskatchewan and California with little resistance and bloodshed; the special forces and Navy SEALs easily took out their respective rebel *policebots*. In Colorado, unfortunately, the governor was ready with ninety-plus rebel *policebots* and three-hundred-plus rebels. The special forces received authorization for satellite assistance. Direct Energy Weapons targeted nearly half the rebel *policebots*. Special forces eliminated a third of the rebels; unfortunately, three friendlies were exterminated. Navy SEALs parachuted in the rear of the rebels, which resulted in an additional third being eradicated. The last third fought to the death, and all the rebels were neutralized; unfortunately, twelve patriots were killed. The military was striving to avoid Abraham Lincoln's axiom: **"America will never be destroyed from the outside. If we falter and lose our freedoms, it will be because we destroyed ourselves."**

In an obscure location in Maine near the Atlantic Ocean, there was an enormous rebel base with a divisional plus force, which was an enhanced division with a couple extra battalions of over six thousand devoted globalists with nine thousand rebel *fighterbots*; Major General Gunner led his troops for an unexpected early-morning attack on Easter Sunday, April 3, 2089. The general commenced the assault with DEWs targeting several soft targets: fuel tankers, armored vehicles, utilities, and suspected headquarters; eighth-generation fighter jets pulverized their designated ground targets with laser weapons.

Next, as the rebels were leaving their barracks, a barrage of guided missiles rained on their positions; high-altitude bombers released their payload on the rebel base. The marines deceptively landed on the ocean side; this caused the rebels to advance to the ocean since the rebels wrongly believed the Navy SEALs were vulnerable. Finally, Major General Gunner, who believed in leading in the front, led his eight-hundred-plus armored vehicles from the west, which was the ultimate combat multiplier; this dominating armored division also possessed friendly soldiers and advanced armored personnel carriers (APCs). This devastating armored unit rolled in and finished off the remaining belligerent rebels, since the enemy had clearly been outflanked. Sergeant Major Nika's sophisticated tank annihilated five rebel armored vehicles; his tank devastated an enemy tank prior to outflanking General Gunner's armored vehicle. The remaining 136 rebels, several of whom were injured, made the correct decision to surrender. Major General Gunner's *Stoic Slayers Task Force* had no casualties; it was a complete slaughter. His stratagem was executed flawlessly. The rebels met their Waterloo.

Sergeant Major Nika expressed, "Major General, you gave the enemy a Hobson's choice. Their limited choices were all failures." Major General Gunner, in his fourth combat tour and his eighth battle victory, was a devoted disciple of Son Tzu, who said: **"All wars are won or lost before they are ever fought."**

The *Stoic Slayers* discovered plans to assassinate President Baros's family and conquer the Capitol. These plans included attacking and destroying Baros Manor and hijacking the *Baros Express*. Clearly, **Mr. Black Rose** was not willing to show any mercy to any of the Baros family members, regardless of age. In addition, **Mr. Black Rose's** plans included violent protests in several major cities; these plans went into great detail. Furthermore, MPs and investigating officers found boxes and boxes of *black roses* and shredded American flags, as well as another *Black Rose* notebook. The intelligence unit was able to hack the rebels' computers and discover other rebel sleeper cells and units, as well as traitorous politicians, which included traitorous nationalists. In addition, devastating evidence was discovered that other globalist countries were involved in the last United States presidential election. This gold mine of evidence was secured for the upcoming military tribunals. Major General Gunner briefed Admiral Davis that, given this intel, he thought this rebellion would be squashed in less than thirty days.

Major General Gunner stated to Admiral Davis, "I have the rebels' plans. I know their vulnerabilities. The *Stoic Slayers*

Task Force will overwhelm the enemy. I know the outcome; if the enemy were wise, which they are not, they would surrender."

In less than two weeks, the *Stoic Slayers Task Force* and friendly forces overwhelmed the rebel forces and decimated over 1,666 rebel lieutenants; this victory occurred because General Gunner knew the rebel tactics and strategies from the hacked information from the rebels' computers and other sources. The rebels' modus operandi did not deviate from *Mr. Black Rose's* established strategies and tactics; Gunner knew their every move. This was their Achilles' heel. General Gunner executed Sun Tzu's principle: **"If you know the enemy and know yourself, you need not fear the result of a hundred battles. If you know yourself but not the enemy, for every victory gained you will also suffer a defeat. If you know neither the enemy nor yourself, you will succumb in every battle."**

The ninety-six rebel lieutenants who surrendered and chose not to fight to the death or take their own lives were sent to Make-Believe Island. Additional enemy evidence was discovered or verified from the captured rebel units and bases; several rebels were willing to provide information in exchange for having the death penalty removed from their sentencing, which included evidence against *Mr. Black Rose*. However, only a few of the captured rebel lieutenants were needed to convict cabal members like *Mr. Black Rose*, as the JAG officers had overwhelming evidence of their crimes. They primarily wanted to negotiate with rebels who had evidence against *Mr. Black Rose* or other cabal leaders. The JAG officers were certain that only a few more plea deals were needed with the captured rebels since they possessed evidence and witnesses to convict the ring leaders like *Mr.*

Black Rose. Additionally, to prevent violating the defendants' rights, the prosecutors made sure not to present any evidence that would create prejudice toward the defendant.

8.

THE TRIBUNALS

NEAR THE END OF APRIL 2089, Admiral Davis was advising President Baros that martial law could end. She believed that Major Gunner's *Stoic Slayers Task Force* had executed *Operation Judgment Day.* First, she informed the president that the targeted suspects had been neutralized or arrested; this included rebel lieutenants and their commanders as well as deep-state rebel operatives. Second, globalist rebel bases within the United States had been removed or were under the control of friendly forces; rebel governors and their respective capitols had been captured. Third, the military should be ready for military tribunals in a few months. Fourth, she expressed that outside enemy forces and countries were not in a position to take advantage of this conflict. Other countries throughout the world were containing or eliminating their respective globalist rebels. In addition, friendly allied forces had reduced the international rebel threat to an acceptable level. Fifth, after meticulous investigation, the military had narrowed the list of suspects to three individuals who could be *Mr. Black Rose.*

President Baros responded, "I concur. Let us broadcast a state of the union address to the people and declare the end of martial law on the agreed-upon date."

Starting in May, the curfew was reduced to 9:00 p.m. to 6:00 a.m., with other requirements similar to those from the beginning of martial law in March 2089. The military and friendly *policebots* controlled the night and continued to mop up the minor rebel resistance. Teresa, Rex, and Sean's school life, including extracurricular activities such as baseball, lacrosse, and Saint Peter's prom, seemed to return to normal. Teresa and her boyfriend Marco went to the Saint Peter prom; she wore a lovely blue dress with her mother's pearl necklace. Marco wore a traditional black tuxedo. Rex and Sofia went to the prom as well; for the last couple of months, they had been dating each other. Sofia was able to visit Baros Manor during the lockdowns. Rex fulfilled all of Sofia's wishes, which included another lovely Mexican dinner on the day of the prom and a dozen red roses; he picked her up in a black limousine. As expected, the Catholic nuns safeguarded that the gregarious prom, which had a Las Vegas casino theme, remained civil and proper; there would be no debauchery or depravity. Teresa and Rex were home before curfew.

The president gave a state of the union address on Armed Forces Day, May 21, 2089; unfortunately, the military and security were on extremely high alert. President Baros declared on all the major networks, "Fellow Americans, we are victorious over the Rebel Forces. Martial law has ended except in a few rebel states; reconstruction shall begin soon in order to bring the entire nation together again; the military will execute *Operation Reconstruction* of conquered globalist states and safeguard this mission's success. The alleged traitors shall be given a just military tribunal; these trials should commence in a couple of months. These trials will be broadcast to guarantee transparency and public trust."

The president continued to reassure the people that law and order would be upheld throughout the land; however, constitutional rights and principles must be true for all, even for the traitors. He reminded them of the words of Will Rogers, an American actor and cowboy: **"We will never have true civilization until we have learned to recognize the rights of others."**

President Baros gave some amazing news and updates. Greenland and Greece had been accepted by the Senate to be the sixty-third and sixty-fourth states. The Summer Games would occur this year; however, they would be in the fall in Athens. He expressed that the lion's share of globalist governments had been defeated and replaced throughout the world. For example, the Philippines and Cuba were liberated after nationalists overthrew their tyrannical governments funded by the globalist cabal and *Mr. Black Rose*. President Baros thanked the Good Lord that no nuclear weapons had been detonated on land; the ones that were launched were vanquished by DEWs. Furthermore, he mentioned that the success of nationalist forces all over the world had been achieved with minimal bloodshed. He reminded all of Sun Tzu's axiom: **"The successful person has unusual skill at dealing with conflict and ensuring the best outcome for all."**

Near the end of the president's speech, Commander Planda and other astronauts gave updates from Mars on their Martian mission; on Earth, the astronauts were nicknamed the first Martian colonists. Planda stated that the two pregnant Martian colonists were doing exceptionally well, and both were expected to have their respective babies in a couple of months or so; two *spacebots* were assisting and monitoring them to guarantee no complications; in addition, Astronaut Julian, a doctor, was monitoring the health of the mothers and their babies. Commander Planda expressed that he remained undefeated in disc golf. He stated that the living area had expanded over sixty acres. The *spacebots* had built a planetarium with an impressive telescope nicknamed the *Cosmos Eye* since it could see the entire known universe. Astronaut Hal delightfully informed the world that they had experienced a few showery days; there was a small lake developing near the astronauts' settlement area. He informed the president that at least two astronauts explored Mars daily. Last month, Commander Planda, with Astronaut Hal, investigated Valles Marineris, which was the largest canyon on Mars; since the Martian atmosphere was significantly improved, they investigated the Martian canyon in a two-man nuclear-powered jet, *NPJ-8*.

Commander Planda thought to himself, *I feel that we living up to Buzz Aldrin's vision when he said:* **"By refocusing our space program on Mars for America's future, we can restore the sense of wonder and adventure in space exploration that we knew in the summer of 1969. We won the moon race; now it's time for us to live and work on Mars, first on its moons and then on its surface."**

On Memorial Day 2089, the Saint Daniel's baseball team was playing in the conference championship; the Roaring Lions had thirty-five wins and eight losses. Sean was pitching in the game. In the fifth inning, with the bases loaded, Sean struck out their best hitter, ending the inning. In the sixth inning, after Sean had struck out three times, he hit a massive homerun on his fourth at-bat with two team members on base. The Roaring Lions won 5–0 and headed to the Division 2 playoff. Teresa was at the game and thought about her brother, Father Teddy. She remembered him saying Babe Ruth's words: **"Every strike brings me closer to the next home run."** Later that day, the family rushed to see Rex and his Saint Peter baseball team. Fortunately, the team won the 3A sectional game; unfortunately, they lost in the regional game to one of their rivals in the following week.

A few days after Memorial Day, the Saint Peter lacrosse team was playing in the state championship at an Indianapolis indoor football stadium against their archrivals, Saint Michael's. After four quarters, the two teams were even at seven goals each; the game would go into sudden-death overtime. At the faceoff, Saint Michael gained possession. Their star player charged toward the goal and cranked a wicked shot; goalie Rex remarkably stuffed it with no goal. Next, Rex launched an impressive pass to baller Chad, who cannoned an unstoppable winning goal: a laser top-shelf shot. Saint Peter's Golden Knights won their first lacrosse state championship. Rex admired lacrosse coach and player Chris Hall, who said: **"Lacrosse seems to be a sport of the future. Maybe it's even become the sport of the now."**

In early June 2089, Rex matriculated at Saint Daniel Catholic University after graduating valedictorian of Saint Peter Catholic High School before his eighteenth birthday. For his assiduous efforts, Rex garnered numerous academic and athletic accolades, which made his parents proud. Rex and his friend Chad were looking forward to joining Saint Daniel's sports teams.

In late June, the Roaring Lions baseball team won the Division 2 regional championship. During the close game, Sean was called in as a relief pitcher in the fifth inning. He struck out the next nine batters; Juan, Mariana's brother, hit a solo home run in the third inning. Unfortunately, they lost in the super-regional. Their team ended with a 37–10 record. The wonderful news was that Sean and Juan graduated on time. Sean and Juan were now mechanical engineers, and Mariana was in her third year in nursing. Sean and Juan started working at the Megadroid Company in an office in Indianapolis for the summer.

Before Sean and Mariana's wedding in July, Teresa and Rex had to complete 4-H. Teresa did her usual painting project, which ended up being the reserve grand champion; Sofia was the grand champion with her portrait of Rex hitting a home run. Rex did his annual aerospace project and earned grand champion. The Baros family held that 4-H brought people together and exemplified Helen Keller's words: **"Alone we can do so little. Together, we can do so much."**

The entire Baros family was at Rex's Eagle Court of Honor held by Troop 108 on June 25, 2089; Troop 108 was a Catholic Boy Scout troop that met at Saint Peter Catholic High School. Rex earned his Eagle rank with three silver palms, his National Medal for Outdoor Achievement, and the religious knot. Rex and Sean had gone on two high adventures together, Philmont and Sea Base. His Eagle project was building a grand chessboard with three-foot-sized chess pieces in Saint Peter Catholic High School Park; in addition, this Eagle project included checker pieces if one preferred to play checkers. The chess pieces and checker pieces were red or blue. The chessboard was black and white. Admittedly, Rex loved playing chess and being on the Saint Peter chess team. In addition, the chessboard was in the center of the park's disc-golf course, which was built by Rex's best friend Chad for his Eagle project; the chessboard was relatively close to Sean's Eagle Scout pedestrian bridge project.

Sofia congratulated Rex with an appropriate kiss and a hug; they were now seriously dating, and Sofia was helping Rex learn Spanish. Sofia congratulated Rex for being accepted to Saint Daniel Catholic University. The Baros family supported the spirit of the words of Lord Robert Baden-Powell, the founder of Scounting, which also inspired Rex to build a park chessboard: **"Scouting is not an abstruse or difficult science: rather it is a jolly game if you take it in the right light. In the same time it is educative, and (like Mercy) it is apt to benefit him that giveth as well as him that receives."**

On Independence Day, President Baros was in DC, Kansas, for the United States' 313th birthday; given the recent war, security was still at a very high level. At the presidential podium of Hexagon Grand Yard, President Baros spoke with candor. "For an extended period of time, America has been under attack by enemies from within. We succeeded in preventing the rebels' ends, which included ending our way of life and canceling the Constitution. However, we must remain resilient and maintain our resolve since this will not be the last test."

The president continued by describing the current state of the union. He emphasized that tribunals should start next month. He warned that the country must remain vigilant since pockets of rebels still existed; however, the vast majority had been eliminated or arrested. He reminded all of the inspirational words of John F. Kennedy: **"Ask not what your country can do for you—ask what you can do for your country."** He also quoted Dwight D. Eisenhower: **"Independence Day: freedom has its life in the hearts, the actions, the spirit of men, and so it must be daily earned and refreshed—else like a flower cut from its life-giving roots, it will wither and die."**

After his inspiring speech, there was an exceptional firework and drone show that ended with jets screeching through the sky as the drones assembled to create lasers and a United States flag in the heavens.

It was the Saturday that the Baros family had been eagerly anticipating. On a beautiful, sunny day, the Baros family departed for the wedding in a magnificent limousine; the date was July 9, 2089. Fortunately, the forecast for the day held no chance of rain. They arrived punctually at the majestic Indianapolis Park, which had hundreds of guests and VIPs waiting for their arrival. Sean and Juan looked sharp in their black tuxedos; they had been best friends since elementary school. They would both attend Saint Daniel Engineering Graduate School.

With his best man, Juan, Sean was standing near Father Savio while waiting for Sean's lovely bride. When the wedding music began, the gorgeous bride, Mariana, in a traditional pearl white dress and wearing a silver crucifix necklace, proceeded down the aisle with her proud father. Father Savio presented a heartwarming religious sermon.

After their vows, Father Savio proclaimed, "As revealed in Mark 10:9: **'What therefore God hath joined together, let not man put asunder.'** May I present Mr. Sean and Mrs. Mariana Baros as husband and wife to all. Sean, you may kiss the lovely bride."

Immediately after the lovely wedding, Mariana and Sean left for a two-week honeymoon in Ireland; they were filled with wanderlust and adventure. They arrived in Dublin and spent a few nights there, experiencing the beauty of the Emerald Isle. Mariana insisted on driving and visiting Blarney Castle and the Cliffs of Moher. At the Blarney Castle, Mariana insisted on kissing the Blarney stone. During their romantic trip, they stayed at several bed-and-breakfasts. At night, they would go to a local pub and enjoy excellent Irish food, such as corned beef and cabbage. Sean loved the pub's family atmosphere while he drank his Irish beer. As they were shopping in Shannon, Sean bought a delightful green Irish shirt for Mariana that had the following Irish blessing: **"May you always walk in sunshine. May you never want for more. May Irish angels rest their wings right beside your door."**

Near the end of July, three ominous high-speed cruise missiles, hypersonic weapons, were heading toward Make-Believe Island. General Gunner ordered space command to immediately demolish the two cruise missiles with DEWs. The third cruise missile could be seen from the island. Fortunately, at the last second, a naval ship took it out. General Gunner and Sergeant Major Nika stood steadfastly outside, facing the incoming cruise missile with their radio operator as the third missile was abolished; the missiles were clearly launched to destroy all evidence against *Mr. Black Rose* and the cabal since *Mr. Black Rose* would be imprisoned on the island in a couple of days. General Gunner reflected the sensibleness of Martin Luther King, Jr.'s words: **"Our scientific power has outrun our spiritual power. We have guided missiles and misguided men."**

The military's stalwart super-maximum prison, called the Traitor Penitentiary, was completed with extensive security and could accommodate approximately five thousand prisoners. The prisoners were separated into single or two-person cells, with a maximum of forty prisoners in a corridor; each corridor had controlled heavy-metal entrances and military police oversight. There were surveillance cameras everywhere; the outer area of the prison was secured with guard towers and drones. They were on a strict daily schedule with minimum deviation. All the prisoners wore an orange uniform and an ankle bracelet that could monitor their exact location. Furthermore, space command was able to monitor all activity on the island.

The next day, inside the Traitor Penitentiary, the rebel prisoners fought each other over their loyalty to *Mr. Black Rose*, resulting in widespread chaos. The two opposing factions emerged as a result of the missile attack. The MPs quickly regained control, and the prison was on lockdown. Five prisoners were eliminated; all were still loyal to *Mr. Black Rose*. The opposition was willing to testify against *Mr. Black Rose* since they believed that he and his followers would sacrifice everyone on the island. Several prisoners recognized the wit of Peter O'Toole, an English film actor: **"There may be honor among thieves, but there's none in politicians."**

The prosecutors and defense were negotiating with several treasonous senators and congressmen in order to obtain witness testimony in order to convict and arrest the rebel benefactors like *Mr. Black Rose*. Congressman Drakos was willing to negotiate, which resulted in him being a target; he realized that his benefactors were willing to slaughter everyone on the island to protect themselves and their interests; he had no desire to die for their benefit. In addition, he was one of the leaders of the prison riot who was against loyalty to *Mr. Black Rose* and other benefactors, since he knew who *Mr. Black Rose* was and knew that he was not on the island yet. After some prisoners attempted to murder him, Drakos was placed in solitary confinement under high security. Unfortunately, two witnesses under protection were murdered by other prisoners in the prison's recreational area. Over time, several treasonous individuals gave testimonials that assisted investigators in convicting the rebel benefactors.

The military tribunals were to start in a few weeks. On Make-Believe Island, the military had a headquarters with over ten thousand servicemen and servicewomen— more than a full division. The navy vessels and naval drones continued to patrol the waters around the island, while jets and satellites ruled the sky and space above. Major General Gunner would be the first commander of military operations on Make-Believe Island. The military base on the island was called *Justice Post*.

Commander Gunner awarded his right-hand man, Sergeant Major Kevin Nika, a Meritorious Medal; the general recognized Sergeant Major Nika for his creative and poignant acrostic poem, "Traitor." General Gunner had already recognized Sergeant Major Nika's heroic actions in combat. The General believed that the sergeant exemplified the words of Samurai Miyamoto Musashi: **"Think lightly of yourself and deeply of the world."**

An acrostic poem spells out a word with the first letter of each line, and the poem must rhyme. The word that it spells out should be the theme of the poem. The poem "Traitor" was displayed at Traitorville Last Estate:

> **T**he zealous traitor wishes our good way of life only ill.
> **R**ebellious, ugly tactics are their favorite military drill.
> **A** traitor's black rose is the chilling symbol of their kill.
> **I**nsurrection with lawlessness is their best-chosen skill.
> **T**raitors abandon our constitution to a godless landfill.
> **O**verthrowing our Federal Republic is their wicked will.
> **R**ebel and patriot sacrificed blood must regrettably spill.

In the first tribunal trial at the beginning of August, Honorable Colonel Nilo Omega was selected as the judge, and twelve officers were chosen as the jury. Lieutenant Colonel Daniel Gomez was the prosecutor; he was a highly respected officer who strongly believed in justice and rights. Prosecutor Gomez thought: *I desire to live by Dwight Eisenhower's words:* **"Though force can protect in emergency, only justice, fairness, consideration, and**

cooperation can finally lead men to the dawn of eternal peace."
Regardless of my biases toward the defendants, we must pledge that
these trials are just and righteous, unlike the corrupt trials of former
President Trump before the 2024 presidential election.

Judge Nilo Omega was extremely cognizant of how divided
the country was. He knew that every word and action during
these tribunals would be scrutinized. He recognized Supreme
Court Justice Louis D. Brandeis's warning and observation: **"Our
government…teaches the whole people by its example. If the
government becomes the lawbreaker, it breeds contempt for
law; it invites every man to become a law unto himself; it
invites anarchy."**

The military tribunals started the second week of August
2089. The first case involved plea deals for cooperative rebels who
were initially charged with treason and other felonies; these plea
deals promised that the death penalty was off the table. The JAG
officers concluded that there was no essential need to negotiate
plea deals with any alleged pedophiles or evil, sadistic individuals.
All plea deals were made with treasonous rebels who had been
blackmailed using honeypots and bribes; they avoided any plea
deals with cabal members and pedophiles. After a lengthy dis-
cussion, Judge Nilo Omega concurred with the defense and the
prosecutor that these seventy-seven rebels should be imprisoned
without parole for twenty or thirty years. In addition, if the rebel
did not honor his or her agreed-upon testimony and cooperation,
then the death penalty or life in prison would be back on the table.
Admittedly, Judge Omega initially had a problem with the plea
deals since he thought they were too lenient; he eventually conceded to the prosecution and defense. He was striving to adhere

to the common sense of Marcus Tullius Cicero: **"The function of wisdom is to discriminate between good and evil."** He also was striving to adhere to the warning from Lysander Spooner, an American philosopher: **"A traitor is a betrayer—one who practices injury while professing friendship. Benedict Arnold was a traitor solely because, while professing friendship for the American cause, he attempted to injure it. An open enemy, however criminal in other respects, is no traitor."**

In one of the several military courts, Judge Nilo Omega was overseeing the tribunal with accused Senator Cain. This case was very similar to many of the other tribunals; in order to expedite the judicial process, at least six tribunals were occurring at the same time. The globalist Senator Cain was accused of treason, pedophilia, and bribery; he was assigned and accepted counsel. After opening statements, the prosecutor, Lieutenant Colonel Daniel Gomez, a seasoned JAG officer, commenced the trial with three eyewitnesses. These witnesses, who were all three convicted criminals with plea deals, testified that Senator Cain attended Make-Believe Island and was observed with underage girls. Next, a major testified that DNA evidence was found in a few of the bedrooms that proved that Senator Cain had exploited an innocent underage girl; her identity would be revealed in later testimonies. Furthermore, surveillance video that was acquired during the successful *Operation Anti-Trafficking* raid of Make-Believe Island exposed Senator Cain entering a room at Make-Believe Castle with an underage girl.

Next, the prosecutor had six witnesses testify that Senator Cain took bribes from China and North Korea in exchange for top-secret information on the United States' plans to advance weapons such as

DEWs. One of the witnesses was a captured Chinese spy who testified that he gave Senator Cain a hundred-million-dollar bribe for top-secret information about the DEW and DLB weapons systems. Moreover, a lieutenant colonel attested that Senator Cain's bank records verified a ten-million-dollar deposit. With money from *Mr. Black Rose*, Senator Cain had secretly funded gain-a-function research and biolabs that produced weaponized viruses, deceptively hiding the funding within congressional bills; all this funding was illegal. These biolabs were playing God; gain-a-function research focused on additional functions for viruses, such as causing cancer or heart disease. One of the jurors thought about Marcus Tullius Cicero's words: **"No wise man ever thought that a traitor should be trusted."**

The defense strived to discredit the witnesses with no success. The defense questioned the teenager, now eighteen, who was sexually assaulted and raped by Senator Cain when she was only fifteen. The young teenager successfully identified Senator Cain and substantiated the evidence against him; her testimony was compelling and revealing; one of the jurors cried while the teenager recalled and described the rape in great detail. After the closing arguments, Judge Nilo Omega instructed the jury before dismissing them to return with a verdict. Judge Nilo Omega thought about Albert Einstein's words: **"The Nuremberg Trial of the German war criminals was tacitly based on the recognition of the principle: criminal actions cannot be excused if committed on government orders; conscience supersedes the authority of the law of the state."**

The unanimous verdict came back: Senator Cain was guilty of all charges and sentenced to death by firing squad. Judge Nilo

Omega ordered, "The verdict has been rendered. The death sentence shall be carried out in thirty days. May God have mercy on your soul. MPs, escort the convicted prisoner to his cell to await execution!"

The defense requested an immediate appeal. Two weeks later, the appeal was denied. After thirty days from the conviction, the execution was televised on all major networks. Justice was served with the message that treason, bribery, and pedophilia would not be tolerated. Judge Nilo Omega mused: *We must study history and realize that nothing is really new under the sun. We must learn from Marcus Tullius Cicero's words: **"The enemy is within the gates; it is with our own luxury, our own folly, our own criminality that we have to contend."***

President Baros pushed Congress to pass a bill to guarantee that all convicted traitors should be recognized as such. In addition, the bill honored all heroes and servicemen and servicewomen mobilized during the 2089 rebellion; the heroes were awarded the *2089 Globalist Rebellion Campaign service medal*. The president succeeded and signed the bill. After a traitor was executed and buried at Traitorville Last Estate, the ceremonial unit placed a *black rose* and white flag near the headstone. The gravestone had the traitor's name as well as their crimes in black lettering. The white flag had only one word: *Traitor*. The gravestone also displayed the prisoner's preferred religion; the lion's share were atheists, and a few were Satanists.

In September, the Summer Games were being played in Athens, which would be their permanent location. The games were under extremely high security, and the police and security guards spoiled the plans of the few sleeper rebel cells. The United States dominated the games; however, several other countries had exceptional accomplishments, such as Japan, who dominated gymnastics and martial arts. President Baros promised that *Games Plaza*, the location of the Summer Games, would continue to improve to guarantee the success of the games.

Sean, who was now in graduate school, was in his last year of eligibility to play college sports since he was injured in his freshman year and red-shirted. As the starting quarterback for Saint Daniel Catholic University, he was able to hand off the football to either Rex or Juan, the starting fullback and halfback, respectively.

In October, the Roaring Lions were playing their conference rival. On their opening drive, Sean had Rex and Juan run the football down the opponents' throats. After thirteen plays and a nine-minute drive, Juan scored a touchdown on an eight-yard run. Starting the fourth quarter with the ball, the Roaring Lions were leading fourteen to nothing. Everyone was expecting Sean to play ball control and kill the clock. In the third play, he surprisingly threw a deep pass to his brother, Rex, who was wide open. Rex sprinted for sixty-three yards for a touchdown. The Roaring Lions were undefeated with six wins and expected to be conference champions for the second year in a row.

After the awesome game, Sean, with his wife, Rex, Sofia, and friends, went out to dinner and dancing to celebrate. The next day, Rex played on the Roaring Lions disc-golf team, which won their fourth tournament in a row. After the competitive victory,

Rex contemplated to himself, *I love playing disc golf because I feel free from the troubles of life and one with God's universe as my disc soars through God's disc-golf course of life to His heavenly basket.*

The Honorable Judge Nilo Omega, who was recently promoted to brigadier general, was overseeing *Mr. Black Rose's* tribunal; this was the judge's ninth tribunal case. *Mr. Black Rose's* identity was revealed: His actual name was Carl Flight, who was well-known to the world and Senator Cain's running mate. He was a well-known hectobillionaire and a political benefactor, and he donated to globalist candidates such as local globalist DAs, judges, congressmen, senators, and presidential candidates. He had established his enormous wealth via speculation and hedge funds. Carl Flight, alias *Mr. Black Rose*, had been accused of economically obliterating countries such as Ireland, Greece, Argentina, and Costa Rica. He was the founder of the Global Community Institute, which supported global initiatives with scientific reasoning and without religion.

After opening statements, a witness, a lieutenant colonel, established hard evidence that Carl Flight, alias *Mr. Black Rose*, owned and oversaw Make-Believe Island; he was a hoary eighty-seven years old, approximately six feet tall with grey hair and a mustache. He managed the facility in order to blackmail and gather evidence against installed politicians, and the evidence was insurance to control the politicians and others. The sinful facility was also used to pay off politicians and others.

The prosecutor, Lieutenant Colonel Daniel Gomez, continued with his first witness. The lieutenant colonel stated, "Every bedroom and exotic entertaining area in the hotel had cameras and listening devices. In addition, *Mr. Black Rose* had access to watch and listen to anyone in any of the rooms; everything was recorded and stored on a master server on the island." The lieutenant colonel explained that DNA evidence and other evidence was stored in an immense secret storage area accessed through the basement down a quarter-mile tunnel.

Five witnesses testified that Carl Flight had been seen with underage girls; however, they could not verify that *Mr. Black Rose* had escorted any girls to a hotel room. On the other hand, they could verify that he had taken girls to his office. Another witness, a major, confirmed that *Mr. Black Rose's* office had a private passageway to a secret bedroom; the uncanny room had several bouquets of *black roses* and portraits of *black roses*. In addition, the major revealed that *Mr. Black Rose's* DNA and the DNA of several young girls had been discovered on the bed in the secret room. These convincing women testified about their respective experiences of statutory rape when they were innocent young girls.

Congressman Drakos, under a plea deal, testified that *Mr. Black Rose* blackmailed him using a Chinese honeypot and money; the honeypot was a gorgeous person who seduced and then spied on another person. The congressman had a relationship with the stunning Chines spy for several years. Congressman Drakos had been directed by *Mr. Black Rose* to vote for Chinese interests, such as voting against Chinese tariffs and against protecting the southern border from illegal Chinese immigrants.

Furthermore, *Mr. Black Rose* insisted on funding anything that played God, such as biolabs creating gain-a-function viruses. These labs were located in several countries, including China and North Korea. Congressman Drakos confirmed that there was a ledger, the *Black Rose Notebook*, that had a list of all the politicians and others being blackmailed and how they were extorted.

Next, twenty credible witnesses, some with plea deals and others not, confirmed numerous bribes, treasonous activities, and extortions of politicians and others. This revealed that *Mr. Black Rose* controlled practically all world globalist leaders via blackmail or bribes; the evidence exposed that he was in the process of creating a new world order that would do anything to eliminate nationalism, traditional families, and Christianity. They confirmed that world leaders and politicians were also subjugated by *Mr. Black Rose*.

A very trustworthy bank auditor testified about the money trail of bribes and blackmail. He revealed several bank transfers from *Mr. Black Rose* to bribed politicians, as well as transfers to *Mr. Black Rose's* bank account of laundered or redirected money for so-called humanitarian aid. Three military financial officers verified the bank accounts and activities, as well as the bank auditor's testimony. They confirmed that money went to United States' enemies like China and North Korea, as well as the purchase of a dirty nuke that was destined for Greenland silver mines; Navy SEALs prevented this evil plan.

Three more witnesses verified that Carl Flight used his nonprofit, Global Community Institute, to launder money to support illegal biolabs throughout the world so that he himself, *Mr. Black Rose,* could play the Almighty. Specifically, these witnesses demonstrated that his nonprofit funded the North Korean bio-lab that developed the Doggam virus that was responsible for the *plandemic*. At the same time, his nonprofit funded pharmaceutical corporations to find a cure; ironically, **Mr. Black Rose** ensured that the pharmaceutical companies were given critical information about the manmade virus. In addition, these virus labs were just about to introduce another virus that would be as deadly as the Black Death, which annihilated nearly half of Europeans in the 1300s; fortunately, the US military spoiled their plans. **Mr. Black Rose** believed that there were too many useless idiots in the world who were just consuming limited resources. Furthermore, the useless idiots could be replaced with *servicebots* and machines.

In November of 2089, Carl Flight, alias **Mr. Black Rose**, was given his last meal and last rights; his last meal was spaghetti and meatballs. He waived his right to see a cleric or priest since he was a devout atheist. This was the third execution for the day; convicted traitors Chief Justice Johnathon Robertson and Judge Richard Pilot were executed earlier. After being escorted to the Traitors' Wall, Carl Flight, alias **Mr. Black Rose**, was blindfolded and placed against the wall that had numerous holes from previous executions. There was a crimson target placed over Carl Flight's heart.

A well-decorated combat veteran colonel read the execution order and ordered Sergeant Major Nika to commence. The sergeant major ordered, "Squad, aim. Fire!"

After the lifeless body collapsed, a medical doctor confirmed that **Mr. Black Rose** was deceased; he had met his coup de grâce. The colonel reflected on Supreme Court Justice Antonin Scalia's legal opinion on the death penalty: **"It's absolutely clear that** whatever cruel and unusual punishments may—may mean with regard to future things, such as death by injection or the electric chair, it's clear that—that the death penalty, in and of itself, is not considered cruel and unusual punishment."

On a somber 2089 Veterans Day, President Baros and his beloved family were at Traitorville Last Estate; Lori was holding baby Theodore. Admiral Sarah Davis, Sergeant Major Nika, and Lieutenant General Gunner, recently promoted, were standing next to the president in their fully decorated uniforms. They all could see that at each traitor's gravestone there was at least one *black rose* and a traitor's flag; this was clearly poetic justice. As the Baros family stood directly in front of **Mr. Black Rose's** gravestone, they could hear in the distance the firing squad executing another convicted traitor. Each one of the Baros family members laid a *black rose* at **Mr. Black Rose's** grave, which had hundreds of *black roses* already, since other victims had come to verify the death of the traitor. The Baroses each then gave a kiss to baby Teddy as they wept for Father Theodore. They each knew that the treasonous rebels had earned their execution.

Before leaving the ominous gravesite, President Baros was pensive: *I pray that God has mercy on your black demonic soul, Mr. Black Rose; however, God knows that I truly desire that you burn in eternal damnation. You have harmed my beloved family and me more than you deserve to know. As president of this great nation, I was obligated to maintain a stoic demeanor when your evil actions murdered my cherished son. Of course, my beloved wife and family mourned deeply for our loss, which tormented my soul. Obviously, your wickedness did not cease with our family; however, out of fairness to you, nothing you did to my family was personal; it was merely diabolical business. You would have committed these malicious acts toward any nationalist president and their family.*

*You sought to end this great constitutional federal republic and erect an Orwellian globalist world order based on lies and immorality. Because of your hubris, you desired to be a deity and Übermensch in order to manipulate our DNA and challenge the one true God. Your sins against man may be forgiven; however, your arrogant desire to be a god is not forgivable. You have clearly violated Mark 3:29: **"But he that shall blaspheme against the Holy Ghost hath never forgiveness, but is in danger of eternal damnation."** You clearly have earned your traitor's black rose.*

ACKNOWLEDGMENTS

I.M. STOICUS would like to acknowledge our older son for inspiring him to write these books and my family for their support and encouragement in becoming a stoic writer. Their encouragement and motivation inspired him to found *Stoic Writing, LLC*; the webpage is **www.stoicwringsllc.com**. In addition, **I. M. Stoicus** would like to thank the exceptional staff of Columbus Publishing Lab, who were terrific in assisting him in creating these books. This encouragement has resulted in three novels: award-winning *HUMAN'S ENHANCEMENTS, ANOTHER WORLD,* and now *TRAITOR'S BLACK ROSE.*

ABOUT THE AUTHOR

I.M. STOICUS is the author of *ANOTHER WORLD* and *HUMANS'* *ENHANCEMENTS* as well as *TRAITOR'S BLACK ROSE. HUMAN'S ENHANCEMENTS,* and *ANOTHER WORLD,* his first and second novels respectively, earned recognition from *Outstanding Creator,* and *Literary Titans.* I. M. Stoicus retired in 2017 as a Lieutenant Colonel with over thirty years of military service; this soldier served as both a combat engineer and quartermaster officer. He is a combat veteran who was deployed or mobilized for nearly eight years in his military career. In 2004, he earned the *Combat Action Badge* and *Combat Patch* during a combat tour. In 2007, he completed his highest military school, *Command and General Staff College.* In addition, he is a Purdue Civil Engineer graduate; in 1994, he was initiated as a Chi Epsilon, National Civil Engineering Honor Society. He has been a practicing engineer for over twenty-eight years. In 2002, he earned his Professional Engineer (PE) license and Professional Traffic Operations Engineer (PTOE) certification. The author has additional degrees in Psychology and Philosophy from Valparaiso University, as well as a Master of Science in Management from Wesleyan University. In 2023, I. M. Stoicus founded *Stoic Writings, LLC*; the webpage is **www.stoicwritingsllc.com**. His beloved family comprises his lovely wife for over twenty-four years and their two Eagle Scout sons.